The Gathering Storm

Daughters of the People, Book 6

LUCY VARNA

The Gathering Storm

Daughters of the People, Book 6

LUCY VARNA

Bone Diggers Press
www.bonediggerspress.com

For you, the reader.
Thank you for your patience during the long lull between books.

Cover design © L.J. Anderson, Mayhem Cover Creations.

Published by Bone Diggers Press, Clayton, Georgia.

ISBN 978-1-943465-36-1

TITLES BY LUCY VARNA

THE DAUGHTERS OF THE PEOPLE SERIES
The Prophecy
Light's Bane
The Enemy Within
Tempered
In All Things, Balance
Sanctuary
The Gathering Storm

THE SONS OF THE PEOPLE SERIES
Say Yes

THE CULLOWHEE HERITAGE SERIES
A Higher Purpose
A Wicked Love

THE PRUXNÆ SERIES
Thief of Hearts
The Choosing
Alien Mine
A Warrior's Touch

One

Sigrid Glyvynsdatter leaned against the bar inside The Omega, Tellowee, Georgia's only nightlife, and sipped her lager. Duke and Carolina were playing hoops on the TV hanging in a corner above the bar. She kept one eye on the game. It wasn't all that interesting, but it beat staring at the people crowded into The Omega. Word had already spread in the close-knit town. Jerusha Mankiller had discovered the bones of two Sisters. For the People, the find might as well have been the Holy Grail.

Carolina scored, and Moira Firebrand shot a triumphant grin at Sigrid. "Three minutes."

Sig snorted and set her mug on the bar's smooth, burled oak surface. "The game isn't over yet."

She wouldn't have worried about its outcome at all if she hadn't bet a night of babysitting on Duke blowing Carolina out of the water. Moira had gone through her needing recently and, of all things, had submitted to the father, Tom Fairfax, and become mortal. Apparently, they were in love. The very idea rankled. If Moira had truly wanted to protect her child and lover, she would never have submitted to him. A Daughter's best strength resided in her immortality, not in her tender heart.

The bartender switched Sigrid's nearly empty mug for a fresh one. She ignored him. Men were one and the same, good to warm her bed for a night or two and not much else. What use was it to get to know one? She had no intentions of falling in love and her needing was months away. Even if she wanted another child, now would be the worst possible time for her to have one. The People were on the cusp of change, positioned on the verge of finally gaining the strength to overcome their greatest enemy. Now of all times, Sigrid needed to concentrate on her duty, not fritter her time away chasing after a handsome face.

Though she'd be the first in line to examine the Sisters' bones, the discovery held only mild interest for her. Extracting DNA, analyzing it, and comparing it to the Institute for Early Cultural Studies' growing database of modern DNA samples was child's play. That she might have a hand in reuniting the People with a significant part of their history excited her not at all.

She tossed her braid over her shoulder and stifled a sigh. At her age, boredom was to be expected. She'd spent centuries doing exactly what she wanted, fighting wars, raiding and pillaging. The pillaging had been fun, especially when it ended with a strapping man chained to her bed.

Good times.

Duke stole the ball and passed it down the court, and one of the guards scored on a beautiful layup. Sig cut a side-eyed glance at her red-headed companion. "Two minutes."

Moira twisted her wide mouth into a grimace. "Feckin' butterfingers."

"Should I say I told you so now or wait until Duke wins?"

"Keep dreaming, you cockeyed Viking."

"I'd rather be cockeyed than knocked up."

Moira whirled around, her blue eyes hot. "No swipes there, Sig, or I'll take ye down a peg."

Sigrid pushed away from the bar and eyed the temper sparking in her friend's eyes. Maybe tonight wouldn't be such a wash after all. It had been ages since she and Moira had gotten into a row, and they always proved interesting. The younger Daughter's fighting tactics were as creative as her language and twice as fun to counter.

The bartender smacked his fingers against the bar, drawing Sigrid and Moira's attention. "No fighting, not tonight."

Moira rolled her eyes and slumped against the edge of the bar, muttering under her breath.

The bartender's finely arched eyebrows furrowed over leaf green eyes. "Don't test me, Moira."

Sigrid hid her humor behind a sip of her lager. As if he had a chance of winning against a Daughter, mortal or not.

Carolina scored, and Moira whooped. "Forty-five seconds."

"You're counting your chickens," Sigrid said.

"That I might be, but at least I know the difference between a bird and a basketball player."

Sigrid slapped her mug onto the bar. "Are you calling Duke's men's basketball team chickens?"

Moira waggled her strawberry blonde eyebrows. "If the shoe fits."

The bartender braced his hands against the edge of the bar. "Why is it that nobody else comes in here and gives me trouble except the two of you?"

Moira flashed a grin at him. "Ye're just lucky that way, cousin."

"More like cursed," he muttered. "No fighting."

He hustled off to fill an order, and Sigrid turned back to the game. The problem was, she *was* bored. Her life had settled into the most humdrum of routines. Get up early, workout, go to work at the IECS. Come home at the end of the day and workout again, then drop by the Omega and snipe at Moira for an hour before the Irish Daughter's husband dragged her home. Where was the adventure, the action, the sheer lunacy of Sigrid's youth? The world had changed in the twelve centuries since her birth, and she didn't like it one bit.

Perhaps a trip to the darkest reaches of Africa might be in order. There were still wars being fought there, plunder for the taking, innocents needing a hand against the hammer of the cruel and unjust. She could wrap up her work at the IECS within six months at the most and hand the remaining details over to her assistant, George Howe. He was intelligent enough, for a man, though a bit bashful for her tastes, and should be able to finish their work on his own with no major glitches.

Moira punched her fists into the air and wiggled her butt. "Carolina wins, and that's a night of sitting when the babe gets here."

"Let's go two for three."

"Oy, there, Sigrid. A deal's a deal and there'll be no wiggling out of it."

"Who's wiggling?"

Moira jabbed her finger at Sigrid's sternum. "That'd be the one, right there."

Sigrid stared down her nose at the smaller Daughter. "I'm a cheat now?"

"Aye and a right good one. Would it kill ye to give me a night out with me Tom?"

Sigrid gritted her teeth together. "I wasn't trying to wiggle—"

Moira's hands bunched into fists at her sides and she stepped up toe to toe with Sigrid, unmindful of the half-foot difference in their heights. "Liar."

Sigrid shoved two fingertips into Moira's shoulder. "Half-wit."

Moira's shoulder twisted around. She popped back into her former position and pushed Sigrid into the person standing behind her. "If I'm a half-wit, ye're a bloody fool, ye lily-livered, fog-brained, goat-faced hag."

Sigrid sucked in a breath. "I am *not* lily-livered. You take that back."

Moira stuck her dainty chin out. "Why don't you make me, ye yellow-spined coward?"

A red haze descended over Sigrid. Nobody called her a coward, *nobody*. She snapped her fist back, preparing to punch. A hard hand wrapped itself around her upper arm, holding her firmly in place. She swiveled around and came face to face with the bartender.

"I said no fighting."

Sigrid yanked at her arm. "Stay out of this, barkeep."

He stared her down, one hand wrapped around her arm, the other loose at his side, his even features set in a hard mask. "My bar, my rules. You don't like them, there's the door."

"Run away now, coward," Moira sneered.

Sigrid jabbed her elbow back and missed. Damn it, where had the little firebrand gone?

The barkeep snagged Sigrid's other arm and yanked her against his chest. "No fighting," he gritted out, and his mouth came down on hers, hot and hard and demanding.

Her anger over Moira's smart mouth evaporated into incredulity. Who did this upstart think he was, assaulting a Daughter of her breeding and reputation? She'd plowed through so many men just like him, she couldn't even remember all their names, and he thought he could tame her with a simple kiss?

The very idea was laughable.

He yanked away from her, breaking the kiss.

She wriggled her shoulders. "Let me—"

"When you calm down," he said, and he slid his mouth across hers again, softer, less urgently.

A slow thrum of heat tripped into her blood. It had been months since she'd allowed a man to kiss her, months more since wicked desire had heated her loins. Perhaps she could give this man a moment more before she lashed out and taught him a lesson. She relaxed against him. Why not? One kiss wouldn't kill her and it would lure him into dropping his guard. She could deal with him after she'd taken her pleasure and pay the requisite fines on the morrow, if the resultant damage was great enough and his kin insisted.

He hummed against her mouth and shifted his grip, one masculine hand cupping her nape, the other at her waist. His lips were supple against hers, giving, and his tongue darted out, testing the seam of her lips.

Heat threaded steadily through her, growing inch by inch, and the noise around them faded. She parted her lips, inviting him in, and gripped his hips over low-waisted jeans. He was warm against her, solid, and patient in his explorations. His tongue dipped into her mouth, teasing her, and he nipped her lower lip.

Desire stuttered to life inside her and her skin tingled. Oh, he was good, so good, and deliciously sweet. She flicked her tongue out. Mint and chocolate mingled together in his mouth, and she tasted him again and again, eagerly sampling what he willingly offered.

His hand tightened on her nape, and a moment later, he eased away and stared down at her, his light green gaze oddly dispassionate. "Next time, you're out."

He let her go and pivoted away, pushing through curious onlookers toward the backroom.

Sigrid staggered into the bar next to Moira. "Pick another fight with me."

Moira snickered. "Aiming to get kicked out?"

"Aiming for another kiss." Sigrid sucked her lower lip into her mouth and tasted him. Mmm. Mint and chocolate. A delightful combination. "Is he taken?"

"Not as I'm aware, though his eyes drift often enough to a certain woman."

Some of the heat ricocheting through Sigrid dissipated. "Who?"

Moira snorted into her water bottle. "Like ye don't know."

"I truly don't. Tell me."

"And give his secrets away? Not a chance."

"At least tell me his name."

Moira shook her head. "Two years, ye've been in Tellowee."

"What does that have to do with anything?"

"Ye've been coming here for two years and still don't know the bartender's name." Moira capped her water. "I'm for home."

"Moira—"

Moira grinned. "Good luck with another kiss."

She slipped through the crowd toward her new husband, and Sigrid glowered after her. First, Moira had called her a liar, then a coward, and now, she refused to name the man that had just kissed Sigrid, her closest friend, near senseless.

And that after winning a bet and earning a babysitter for a night a few months hence.

Sigrid put her back to her friend's bouncing step and hunched over her lager. It just showed that a Daughter was better off relying on herself, or would if Moira weren't such a hotheaded, fickle creature. Help one minute, fight the next, and no one could predict which one would come first or what the outcome of either would be.

The backroom's door smacked open and Sigrid glanced up. A young blonde strode out carrying a tray of plated food. The door paused in mid-swing. Beyond it, Sigrid could just make out the kitchen and another door, that one tightly shut. An idea blossomed in her head. She set her lager down and glanced around. The waitress had her back to Sigrid and was setting steaming entrees in front of women sitting at a table on the other side of the room.

Sigrid slipped quickly through the crowd gathered near the bar and into the backroom. An efficiently organized commercial kitchen spread out to her left. One person manned the grill, a rangy, middle-aged man wearing a grease stained apron over a black t-shirt and jeans.

"Help you?" he asked.

Sigrid jerked her thumb at the closed door. "I need to speak with the bartender."

The man shrugged and flipped a burger. "He's probably in his office. Through that door, down the hall, second door on the left."

Sigrid inclined her head once. "Thank you."

She twisted the doorknob, pushed the door open, and

headed toward the intriguing young man who had dared to steal a kiss from an immortal Daughter.

WILL CORBIN sank into the cushy chair behind his desk and raked trembling hands through his hair. He'd kissed Sigrid, really kissed her, and blessed Ki, it had been good. After the first kiss, she'd relaxed and opened for him, kissing him back exactly the way he'd been dreaming she would for nearly two years now. Heat thrummed through his blood and his dick stood at half mast. Sweet mercy, if he had his way, he'd go back out there right now, haul her into the nearest private room, and kiss her a third time, just so he could linger over the delicious fit of her mouth against his.

She was probably ready to kill him. It wouldn't be the first time a Daughter skewered a man who touched her without her explicit permission. Probably wouldn't be the last, either. Most Daughters had a very low tolerance for men in general, Sigrid even less.

He launched himself out of his chair and paced around his battered desk. What had he been thinking, assaulting her like that? If she didn't kill him, and that was a likely outcome, she could sue him and ruin the business his parents had worked so hard to build. He halted in front of the worn, leather sofa set to one side of his office and stared at the family pictures dotting the wall above it. His parents on their wedding day. Them holding him between them in front of the newly-opened Omega. Him and his youngest sister kneeling on stools in front of the bar.

Years of sweat and labor and love, gone in one, impulsive caress.

Maybe he would've acted differently if he hadn't wanted her for so long.

He pivoted and paced in the other direction, skirting the two rickety chairs set in front of his desk. The soles of his running shoes thudded quietly against the thin, institutional gray carpeting, keeping time with the irregular thump of his heart.

Yeah, maybe he wouldn't have grabbed her if he hadn't already been on edge, over the unexpected crowd, over his ongoing inability to attract Sigrid's attention, over her and Moira fighting *again*. It wasn't an excuse, no. He should've handled that pair the way he usually did, with the swift crack of his baseball bat against the edge of the bar. Instead, he'd given in to his frustration and yanked Sigrid into a kiss.

He stared blankly at the equal opportunity employment posters decorating the wall in front of him. He'd kissed her in front of half of Tellowee, people she'd likely known for far longer than he'd been alive. If word got out, she'd never live it down. Other Daughters would tease her mercilessly for years about giving in to him.

He groaned and clapped his hands over his face. Yup, she was gonna kill him.

The door opened behind him and he dropped his gaze to the floor. "I'm busy."

The door snicked shut and a cool, feminine voice said, "I see."

Sigrid. Well, shit. Good thing he kept his last will and testament up to date. He turned slowly, hands loose at his sides, gaze steady. "Will it do any good to apologize?"

She arched one blonde eyebrow. "Do you regret kissing me?"

"No."

"Then why apologize?" She strolled slowly toward him. Her hips swayed gently with each long stride and her booted feet were silent along the carpeted floor. "Perhaps I enjoyed it."

He kept his mouth shut and waited for her to strike.

She stopped a foot away from him. "Or perhaps I've come to teach you a lesson."

"Then do it outside. I don't want my sister to have to clean up my blood."

"A realist or a fatalist?"

"Maybe a little of both. Look, just do whatever you're going to do and get it over with."

"So eager to meet justice at my hand." She stepped closer and rested her palms on his chest over the unsteady thud of his heart. "What if I offered you another option?"

He looked at her then, really looked at her for the first time since she'd entered the room. Her steely blue eyes were shuttered, her rosy lips slightly parted, and the pale skin over her high cheekbones was flushed. Her long, golden braid fell over one shoulder. Its tip teased the top of her breast through her fitted, deep blue sweater. She hadn't worn her sword tonight, but that didn't mean she wasn't carrying a weapon. She probably had a handgun tucked against her back in the waistband of her jeans or a knife at her ankle, maybe both.

On the other hand, she was a Daughter, trained to fight from her first step on. She didn't need weapons to dismantle him limb from limb.

He knotted his hands into fists as his sides, keeping them exactly where they were and not where he wanted them to be, on her. "Stop playing with me."

She rocked onto the flat heels of her boots and walked around him, trailing her fingertips along his shoulder and across his back. "Who's playing? You allowed me to sample you."

"No, I kissed you to keep you from killing Moira."

Sigrid laughed. "You truly think I'd kill her?"

"The way the two of you go at each other? Yeah." He shrugged, hoping to dislodge her fingers and the tingling warmth spreading over his skin under them and his button-down shirt. "She's a pain in the ass, but she's my cousin. I couldn't let you hurt her."

"So you did it out of love. I wonder, barkeep. What else would you do for love?"

He ground his teeth together. Why did older Daughters always have to play their little games? "That's not really any of your business."

"Isn't it? Hmm." She finished her circuit and faced him again. "Tell me your name and perhaps I'll forgive your indiscretion."

"Seriously?"

"Of course. Tell me."

Disappointment throbbed through him. Two years and she didn't even know his name. He shook his head and backed slowly away from her. "Forget it. You want to kill me for touching you, go ahead. Otherwise, I have a business to run."

Anger sparked into her eyes, warming them to a deep blue. "You're refusing me? I could break every bone in your body before you could mount a suitable defense."

"You could try."

"And now you challenge me." She lifted her chin and met his gaze evenly. "I'll know every detail of your young life within half an hour of leaving The Omega."

Every emotion she'd stirred drained out of him. Fat chance of that. If she didn't know his name by now, no way in hell would she bother digging into his life. He'd overheard her direct one too many callous remarks at the men she'd discarded one by one over her long, long life to believe otherwise.

"Are you ready for an apology now?" he asked.

"Moira and I were spoiling for a fight. You diffused a tense situation in a way that harmed no one. Unless you regret your actions, an apology is unnecessary."

"Fair enough."

Her eyes narrowed into blue slits. "Half an hour."

He managed a small smile. "Yeah, right. Go on, now. Tell Casey to get you another lager before you go, on the house."

"Perhaps tomorrow." She dipped her head in a respectful bow. "Well met, barkeep."

He returned her bow. "Well met, Sigrid Deathknell, daughter of Glyvyn the Ice Warrior, of the line of Bagda."

She studied him solemnly for a long moment, then pivoted sharply and marched out of his office. Will leaned a hip against

11

the edge of his desk and admired her fluid gait. By Ki, she was beautiful, but it was past time for him to let go of the crush he had on her and move on. There had to be another woman out there who was eager for his love. He'd just have to work harder at finding her, and maybe he would. Just as soon as he forgot how good it'd felt to kiss the woman of his dreams.

Two

Sigrid unlocked her front door and flipped lights on as she wandered through her house. The three-story, brick Victorian was hell to maintain, but its size and cozy rooms were perfect for her needs. Here, her family could visit whenever they wished, stay as long as they liked, and never interfere with her privacy.

She trailed a hand over the antique Chippendale settee in her office, then settled into the sleek, ergonomically designed chair behind her desk and booted up her laptop. That hadn't always been the case. The first two centuries of her life had been rough. She'd lived hand to mouth, hired her sword arm to foreign princes and the occasional queen, took work whenever she could find it, and otherwise did whatever she had to do to survive. It was a typical life for an immortal Daughter, even now in the luxurious golden age of affordable technology and easy access to work.

A few well-placed taps on the keyboard and the tax assessor's website popped up in the browser. Sigrid input the address for The Omega and waited patiently for the results. If Moira had told her the young barkeep's identity, it wouldn't be necessary to snoop on his parents, the most likely owners of the tavern he worked in. Stubborn Irish was getting a little big for her breeches.

The search netted one entry. Sigrid clicked into it and frowned. The owner was listed as Wilhelmina Corbin, and Sigrid knew of only one Daughter with that given name. Wilhelmina the Fierce was a child of Anya Bloodletter, a member of the Council of Seven representing the line of Abragni, the youngest of the Seven Sisters.

Sigrid relaxed into her chair and drummed her fingertips on the top of her desk. Anya was younger than her by sixteen years. They'd joined forces often in the first few heady decades of their lives, battling marauding armies, reaping precious bounty, sharing the spoils of their labor.

Men being the primary spoil.

Assuming the barkeep was Wilhelmina's son and, by extension, Anya's grandson, he would be under the protection of women who knew Sigrid by personal acquaintance rather than rumor. Anya would protest a dalliance on that knowledge alone. A permanent alliance in the form of a concubinage or marriage would be welcomed by the councilmember, given their longstanding friendship, but Sigrid was far from wanting one, even as tempting a figure as the barkeep cut.

But that kiss.

She touched her fingertips to her mouth and smiled at the memory of his caress. Masterful, patient, delicious. Would he offer her another at their next encounter, or would she be forced to maneuver him into one?

Unwelcome memory surfaced. Moira had said the barkeep had his eye on a woman. If so, what was he doing kissing *her* instead of pursuing this other female? Would his interest in another forestall his involvement with Sigrid?

She swiveled her chair around and pushed out of it. What did it matter? She could claim him on the kiss alone, by dint of the People's long-standing traditions concerning the management of male progeny. Whether she wanted to or not was another matter entirely.

Now that she knew his probable family, she could discover

his name through the People's extensive genealogies, currently maintained by Robert Upton, the husband of another battle-hardened acquaintance, Rebecca the Blade, one of Anya's nieces. Until then, Sigrid could bide her time. Patience was a warrior's companion, determination her abiding strength. The barkeep would be in her grasp sooner or later, and when he was, perhaps he could be coaxed into sharing more than a simple kiss or two.

WILL WOKE UP with an aching hard-on and the memory of Sigrid's kiss lingering on his mouth.

He cursed under his breath and buried his face in his pillow, ignoring the painful throb of his dick pressed into the mattress. Sleep had eluded him while his mind flirted with tasting her again, touching her, her fingers gliding around his shoulders as she studied him.

Friggin' Daughters and their friggin' games. Maybe he would've been ok if she hadn't put her hands on him. Maybe then he could forget her the way he ought to and start moving on with his life.

He shoved Sigrid out of his mind and threw the covers back. The air in his apartment chilled his heated skin, doing not a damn thing to ease his hard-on. He padded into the bathroom, brushed his teeth while he waited for it to wilt. Remembered the smooth stroke of Sigrid's fingers on his shoulders and cursed the blood surging into his groin.

Two years he'd been playing this game. He spat toothpaste out, rinsed his mouth, patted it dry, and avoided the grumpy stare of his reflection in the bathroom mirror. Futile to keep hoping. Hadn't he decided that on Friday? Futile to dream, futile to want, and yet there it was, a grinding need built deep into his bones.

It was the quickest he'd ever broken a resolution before and it didn't sit well with him. A Son should have more discipline than that, especially where women were concerned, and most especially when a Daughter entered the picture.

A sharp rap on his front door interrupted the downward spiral of his thoughts. He heaved a sigh, snagged a pair of shorts on his way through the bedroom, and loped into the living room.

A lightly accented feminine voice called, "Will?" and he froze where he stood, half into his living room, naked as the day he was born with a pair of loose-fitting gym shorts hanging from one hand.

Sigrid.

Questions swirled through his mind, eddying into a torrent of anticipation and curiosity. What was she doing at his apartment? How had she even found him? Why had she bothered after ignoring him for so long?

Only one way to find out.

He shimmied into his shorts and jogged to the door, swung it open before remembering the hard-on he still sported and the fact that he hadn't washed his face, combed his hair, or put on deodorant.

His first look at her drained every other concern out of his mind. She was a cool breath of fresh air dressed in a slim, ivory skirt and a tailored navy button down under an ivory colored wool coat. Her toned legs ended in heels the same color as her shirt, putting her on eye level with him. He slouched against the doorframe and looked his fill, reveling in the light musk of her perfume, the filtered sunlight glinting off her golden braid, the perfectly arched eyebrow she aimed at him.

"Will Corbin?"

"Yeah." And just to be contrary, he crossed his arms over his chest and let the cold, winter air wash over him, raising goose bumps on his skin. She was there, sure. Didn't mean he had to let her in, though he'd be a fool not to, if only to satisfy his curiosity. "What can I do for you?"

She waggled the small paper bag she held in her gloved hand. "DNA sample. Everyone needs to be tested."

He shrugged. "And?"

"You haven't been."

Which he by golly already knew. He'd received a kit in the mail weeks ago and tossed it on his kitchen counter with a pile of other junk mail, where it rested still. And damn it all, he should've already gotten around to taking care of that. Duty demanded it of him, to his family, to his People, to the need they had to preserve their heritage and keep themselves safe from an ever dangerous world.

On the other hand, if he'd sent the sample back already, he might not've ever had the pleasure of standing across from the woman of his dreams while wearing nothing but a pair of gym shorts.

"Simpler to mail a reminder," he said.

"Simpler, yes. Not as rewarding as a personal visit." Her icy eyes flicked down his body and back up again, and a small smile tilted her luscious mouth. She nodded toward the interior of his apartment, a regal tilt of her head. "May I?"

Oh, yeah, she could. He stepped back, welcomed the brush of her coat against his bare, chilled skin, shut the door behind her. She sauntered into the room, cool demeanor firmly in place, every inch a war-hardened Daughter as she surveyed his living room. Cushy leather sofa set squarely in the middle of the floor next to a glass-topped coffee table, the row of bookshelves against the far wall, the entertainment center housing his TV, the movies and games stacked untidily around it.

The fine layer of dust, the empty beer bottle he'd neglected to recycle last night, and his gym shoes and socks thrown on the floor, exactly where he'd left them.

He scowled at them. Good thing his mother was out of the country. She'd skin him for inviting a woman into his apartment when it wasn't picture perfect.

But hey, at least the original landscapes dotted along the eggshell colored walls were straight. The dust on their frames was hardly noticeable from where they stood.

Sigrid turned in a slow half circle and stopped, facing him. "Very nice."

He nearly heaved a sigh of relief. Great. She hadn't noticed the dust. "It's home. Can I get you something? A coke or some water?"

"I'm fine, thank you." She handed him the paper bag, stripped off her gloves, and shrugged out of her jacket, patiently exchanged her outerwear for the bag, and waited for him to hang the jacket on the hook by the door. "This won't take long. Do you have plans for lunch?"

He paused with his hands on the sleeves of her coat, in the middle of smoothing them out. "Ah, no. Why?"

"You do now. Sit."

"Wait."

He scrubbed a hand over his hair, mussing it as he rewound the conversation through his befuddled mind. Sigrid knocking on the door, his hard-on still hard, DNA kit and polite niceties, the whiff of her perfume teasing him where it lingered in the air. Nothing about a meal. Hunh. Maybe he'd missed something.

"What plans do I have again?" he asked.

"Lunch. Unless you prefer an evening date."

"I have to work," he murmured. "Are you asking me out?"

Her mouth quirked up at one corner. The half smile softened her icy beauty. "I'm not asking. Sit, Will. I'm expected at work soon."

She wasn't asking.

A tiny thrill pulsed through him. She wasn't asking for a date. She was telling him what she expected him to do, as if she had any right to control his actions. He inhaled a shaky breath and walked to the couch on legs that weren't quite steady. Sank into the plush leather, tried to reel in the hope poking through two years of rejection, and failed.

Who was he kidding? It was a dream come true. He'd be a fool not to grab hold of her interest while it lasted and enjoy every single moment he could before she discarded him and sent him on his merry way.

She pulled medical gloves out of the bag and snapped them

into place on her slim hands. "Have you a preference among the local restaurants?"

He shook his head, too stunned to respond around his hammering heart and the heat coursing through his blood.

"What time does your shift start tonight?" she asked.

"Two." He shook his head again, attempting clarity, and was unsurprised when it eluded him. "I have to be on the floor by three, but I usually go in an hour or two early to deal with paperwork."

"An early lunch then. Franklin?"

"Yeah," he said, and grinned. This was really happening. Sigrid really wanted to go out with him. Hot damn and hallelujah. Sometimes the Great Mother did answer prayers. "There's this place on the Highlands Road. Makes great pizza."

"Pizza it is." She pulled the kit out of the bag, dug into it, extracted a cotton swab sealed in paper, and ripped it open. "Open wide. A good scraping ensures we won't have to do this again."

He obliged, opening his mouth and waiting patiently as she positioned herself between his widespread knees, leaned forward, and rubbed the swab along the inside of his cheek. He fixed his gaze on her face and not on the hint of cleavage peeking through the drape of her shirt. Her scent washed over him, just as tempting as the view, and he closed his eyes, willing his body to behave.

She stepped away, snapped her gloves off, then brushed cool fingers along his jaw. "Look at me, Will."

His eyes flew open and met the brilliant blue of hers. She was close, so close her light breaths feathered along his mouth and the end of her long braid tickled his chest. For a moment, he thought she might close the distance between them and kiss him, and his heart leapt into his throat, hoping against hope for another kiss, another touch, anything to sustain him until he could see her again.

At lunch. On a date. Just him and her.

She scratched her fingernails gently along his jaw and stood. "Meet me at my office at eleven."

"Yeah. Ah." He cleared the thick gravel coating his throat and tried again. "I'll be there at eleven sharp."

"Good." Her luscious mouth tilted into a full smile, sparking humor in her eyes. "Be ready for my full attention."

He stifled a groan, but just barely. Her full attention? Holy cow. What was she trying to do, make him cum right then and there? She might as well have stroked her hand over his dick; her words hit him that hard.

She gathered the kit together and strode toward her coat hung near the entrance. "Don't get up. It would be a shame not to enjoy your arousal while it's fresh."

Rampant need shot through him, shoving him close to an orgasm. Sweet Mother. Sigrid was deliberately stirring him up. And that's what he got for letting her in the door while wearing a thin pair of gym shorts over his morning hard-on.

He clapped his hands over his face and ignored the soft sounds of her shrugging her coat on and leaving. Oh, he was in for it now, and he had no one but himself to blame. That kiss. Two years of wanting her, of biding his time trying to catch her eye, and a hotheaded, impulsive kiss was what she noticed.

Maybe he should've tried that sooner.

He snorted out a laugh and, resigned, eased the elastic waistband of his shorts down over his throbbing erection and stroked a firm fist along its length. Pleasure shuddered through him, rolling along in a steady grind under the lingering musk of her perfume tickling his nose and the remembered feel of her skin on his, and he lost himself in the possibilities she'd opened when she'd stepped through his front door.

Three

Rebecca Upton stood quietly at the head of the conference table, one hand loose along the top of her chair as the Council of Seven and their respective retinues filed into the room. She nodded to each councilmember in turn, and was greeted in kind.

Mutual respect earned over centuries of battle and kinship, centuries dominated by a blood feud with the Shadow and the loss of so much knowledge of their own origins. And now, they might truly be on the verge of rediscovering those origins and of having within their grasp a means of ending a never-ending war.

Hawthorne the Beheader, now the de facto head of the line of Bagda, gifted Rebecca with a rare smile as she took a spot near the middle of the table. Love had mended that one's heart. Few deserved it more or had worked so hard to obtain it.

A thin slice of pain struck Rebecca's heart. Robert, her own love, had been found only after a millennium of searching. Their life had never been perfect. No couple's was, but it had been close, so damn close, and now, that near-perfect life was being threatened. Robert was hiding something from her. She knew him too well not to recognize the signs. She'd have to push him about that, later when he couldn't bury himself in work or the ever demanding needs of their growing family.

And she'd have to tell him. About the vision given to her by the Woman with No Face, and of the Woman's words. About the possibility that Rebecca's long life might be drawing to a close, and with it, their marriage.

Robert would be philosophical. The disease eating away at his muscles lent him that calm, but Rebecca could find no peace in the possibility of living eternally at his side after their respective deaths. It wasn't her nature. It wasn't in her blood. The People were fighters. They had to be, and among them, the Blade was one of their greatest warriors.

Her hand tightened on the chair. Lukas Alexiou might be her doom, but damned if she'd go down without a fight.

Lydia Truthteller of the line of Kiya, eldest of the Seven Sisters, settled into a chair at the opposite end of the table, directly across from Rebecca. "Is it true? Has the Oracle been named?"

"Nala, the name given by our blood enemy." Rebecca pulled out her chair and sat amid the concerned murmurs passed from one ear to the next around the room. "She responds only to the Shadow and only in a language so ancient, it has largely been forgotten by us all."

"Or was never known to us." Hawthorne's gray eyes remained placid as she fixed her gaze unwaveringly on Rebecca. "How did Alexiou come by this language?"

"He will not say." Or was waiting for the People to offer the appropriate price for such knowledge. Who could tell what game the Shadow Enemy's leader played? Even the canny Alexiou seemed not to know. Rebecca delicately cleared her throat and continued. "Business called him home to New York. He has asked my leave to return and visit Nala again."

Miriam of the Nine, an immortal Daughter of the line of Marnan, leaned forward and said, "You will allow this?"

Rebecca nodded. "Until we can find a way to communicate with the Oracle, I feel we must."

"So be it," Lydia said, her rich voice flat. "While he caters to the Oracle's whims, we will use the time to learn everything we can of him and the Shadow."

Eleanor Shadowfell, of the line of Ganenda, the next youngest of the Seven, placed her palms flat on the table, covering the bound agenda laid open in front of her. "Learn of him, yes, but caution must always be exercised when dealing with a man as dangerous and unpredictable as Lukas Alexiou."

A shiver snaked down Rebecca's spine, followed by cold dread as the Woman's words whispered through her mind. *The Shadow approaches and the Blade must yield.* A vision of her sword's blade shattering under the crushing weight of a formless shadow. Her death, foretold. Of everyone there, Rebecca knew without a doubt exactly how dangerous the Shadow could be.

"Is it true his hold on the Shadow is weakening?"

Rebecca focused on the speaker, her aunt Anya Bloodletter, the embodiment of Abragni, the youngest of the Seven, on the Council. "Unconfirmed rumors."

Anya's cornflower blue eyes crinkled at the corners in a half smile. "So that young buck Drew Martin didn't beat the shit out of Marco Alexiou?"

"A just retaliation," Rebecca countered. An unsanctioned retaliation, true, but a just one. The People couldn't run around exacting Retribution Willie nilly, even if this one had been earned by Lukas's younger brother. Marco and their uncle Pinico had captured Rebecca's next youngest daughter Jerusha and tortured her for days while Drew, Jerusha's lover, had tracked them down.

As soon as Jerusha was safely home, Drew had taken three men, a small army given their military training, and meted out revenge on Marco. Rumor had it he was recovering in hiding, but even in hiding, Lukas's deranged younger brother could cause trouble.

Given the Oracle's affinity for Lukas, now was the worst possible time for turmoil among the Shadow Enemy. As long as Lukas remained in control, as long as Nala favored him, he could be swayed to the People's ends. They had no such hold over his younger brother. If Marco was indeed straining at the bit, the resulting upheaval could spell serious trouble for the People, right when the Prophecy of Light was on the verge of being fulfilled, allowing the People to conquer their blood enemy and forever after live in peace.

Rebecca sat back in her chair and allowed her gaze to touch on each of the seven women gathered around the table, there representing the descendants of each of the Seven Sisters, the progenitors of the People. "We now have control of three of the Bones of the Just. One set was found in a nightclub in Gainesville. My daughter Jerusha smuggled the second set of remains out of Turkey recently, and not long after, I sent a team to retrieve the third set from a museum in Boston."

Lydia nodded and a small smile warmed her dark eyes. "And we search for the remaining four. What news?"

"I've assigned a team of IECS scientists to the task, led by Sigrid Glyvynsdatter." Rebecca caught Anya's satisfied nod out of the corner of her eye and a fraction of the burden weighting her down lifted. "She asked me to press each of you again to have every single member of your lines return the DNA tests she mailed to them. Each returned test adds to our knowledge and can help us identify the remaining Bones of the Just."

Agreeing nods and softly voiced assents passed around the room. Rebecca held up one hand, halting the rising excitement. The Bones of the Just, the name given to the skeletal remains of the Seven Sisters, were important relics of the People. Having them gathered in one location after millennia of not knowing where they were would rally the People behind any cause. If ever such accord was needed, it was now.

"There's more," she continued. "We now believe the mention of the Bones of the Just within the Prophecy indicates that wherever they are gathered becomes the People's ultimate Sanctuary."

The tide of conversation rose over Rebecca's remaining words. She sat back and yielded to it, and to the hope underlying each voice, a hope she clung to even as worry remained a stalwart beacon in her mind.

SIGRID SAT at her desk studying a printout of DNA sequencing taken from a recent saliva swab. Thanks to the discovery of the first set of the Bones of the Just some months earlier, funding had been provided to expand the onsite lab facilities. She'd cleared out a room, ordered the necessary equipment, and recruited technicians to expedite processing the hundreds of samples flooding into her office.

Everyone was being tested and retested, Daughters mortal and immortal, Sons, and those having frequent contact with the People.

The printout of the sample she was studying contained mitochondrial DNA of the same haplogroup and pattern as the descendants of the Sisters. Sigrid flipped to the lead page of the report and checked the sample's origins.

James Edward Terhune. Interesting.

She closed the report and stuck it in her outbox for filing, then selected another report and centered it on the calendar aligned precisely on the top of her desk. It wasn't unusual to find a genetic commonality between an outsider and the People. The pre-agricultural human population had been small, and while genealogical and other records for that era didn't exist, there were plenty of records from later time periods. Combined with lore, oral and written, such connections could be found, and often were.

Finding a direct maternal link to the Sisters among outsiders was far less common. Mitochondrial DNA was passed down only in the maternal line. Children born to Sons carried the mitochondrial DNA of their mother, and Sons didn't always marry Daughters. Mortal descendants of the People were only tracked for a few generations before their lines were considered outside the People's close kinship.

How far back would James Terhune's maternal line need to be traced in order to pinpoint his exact relationship to the People?

A soft knock rapped on her door, drawing Sigrid's attention to the entrance of her office. George Howe, her young, mortal assistant, stood in the doorway, shifting from foot to foot. His eyebrows were furrowed beneath a cap of golden hair, his mouth was turned down at the corners, and his clothes were wrinkled and ill-fitting.

She eyed him again from head to toe. Had his clothes always hung so loosely on his sturdy frame?

George shuffled half a foot inside her office, still frowning. "I've got the latest batch of test reports."

Sigrid waited for him to continue. The reports weren't urgent. She usually picked them up on her way through the building and scanned them during lulls in other work, as she'd been doing before George interrupted her.

When he simply stood there filling space she'd rather remain empty, she arched a single eyebrow.

He flushed and hunched his shoulders underneath the worn shoulders of an old sweater. "You've got some messages."

"And?"

"Director Upton called and said she'd reminded the Council of Seven about the DNA tests." He shifted his grip on the reports he was holding, fumbling them as his hands shook, and fished out a yellow post-it note. "Will Corbin called and said he might be a few minutes late. An emergency at the Omega?"

Sigrid folded her hands on the desk and willed her patience to hold. "You are not my secretary, Mr. Howe."

He glance down at the floor, failing to hide the flush staining his cheeks. "No, ma'am."

"You're my assistant, and my assistant is not paid to ferry messages to me."

"No, ma'am."

His voice was quiet, cowed, and for a moment, anger spiked

through Sigrid. Where was this boy's spine? Where was his fortitude? No Son would ever bow under the gaze of another as this one did. No Son would whimper his fear, whether he felt it or not, and no Son would stand quivering in the face of her fury.

But George was not a Son.

Sigrid clamped down on her anger and ruthlessly quashed it. This young man was a brilliant geneticist. She'd handpicked him from among dozens of candidates. That he was timid and weak detracted not one whit from his genius, and though those characteristics annoyed her no end, George showed no signs of overcoming either.

After months of living among the People, shouldn't he have?

She deliberately unclenched her fists and rested her hands flat on her desk. Losing her temper would do no one any good and would ruin the good mood Will had put her in earlier when he'd answered his door wearing only shorts over a body honed by years of disciplined exercise.

"Why are you here?" she asked, deliberately softening her voice.

George lifted his head, and for a moment, stark emotion filled his expression. Before Sigrid could pinpoint it, he shook his head and held up the stack of files and papers clasped in his hands. "We've finished testing the Boston skeletal remains."

He scurried to her desk, dropped his burden in an untidy pile on one corner, and left without once looking her in the face again, nearly bumping into Will on his way through the door.

Will smiled at George and said, "Hey, man," but George ignored him and walked rapidly away, each step a sharp staccato against the tiled hallway floor.

Will's smile faded. He turned to her and jabbed a thumb over his shoulder. "What's eating him?"

Sigrid refused to feel one iota of guilt. Young Howe needed to toughen up, else he'd never survive among the People, and she needed him here, needed his brilliant mind and keen insight.

27

She rose and retrieved her suit jacket from a hanger in the closet tucked away to the side of her office, adjacent a small bathroom. "Are you ready?"

Will gazed at her for a long moment, his green eyes far too shrewd for a man of his relative youth. After a moment, he nodded. "Sure. I'll drive."

Humor rose, erasing the lingering annoyance over George's cowering attitude, and she graced Will with a grin. This one, now, he was a Son. Strong and sharp, confident and a touch arrogant. This man had earned her grace through the kisses he'd dared to steal from her, and so, she would afford him a simple boon.

"All right," she said. "My car or yours?"

If she'd surprised him, it didn't show. His expression remained open and calm, pleasing her all the more.

"Yours." He stepped forward and took the jacket from her, then held it out and helped her put it on. His hands lingered on her shoulders, cupping them as he held her gently, her back to his front. "You smell like heaven."

Pleasure rippled through her, tightening her muscles. His touch warmed her in a way no man's had in decades. She leaned back ever so slightly into his heat, savoring it and the male closeness she'd forsaken for far too long. "Let me get my purse."

He pressed a soft kiss to the side of her throat, a fleeting slide of his lips across her skin, and let her go, and she trembled under the simple touch. For a moment, fear flooded through her. *Danger*, it shouted, *run*, and she almost gave in to it, almost turned and fled from the man who'd captured her attention so thoroughly.

Immediately, she shook the feeling off. No Daughter ran from a man regardless of the circumstance. This man, with his piercing gaze and tempting heat, posed no threat to her. She would take what she wanted from him and, in accordance with the laws of the People, discard him when she was finished. After, she would remain cold and heartless, as all good Daughters were.

Four

Sigrid's car handled like a dream.

Will downshifted through the curves defining the road leading into town. The purr of the Porsche Boxster's engine reverberated through the steering wheel into his left hand, a reminder of the manmade machine's power and grace.

Traits it shared with its owner.

He cut an admiring glance at his companion out of the corner of his eyes. Sigrid relaxed into the passenger's seat with her hands folded primly in her lap. Her long, shapely legs were crossed at the knees under the elegant lines of her ivory skirt.

That skirt had seemed so demure in her office. It fell to precisely six inches above the center of her knees. Yet here, with her sitting in the car beside him, it rode up, exposing another four inches of her shapely thighs, a sinful temptation juxtaposed against her composed, icy beauty.

He shifted in his own seat, easing the first stirrings of lust in his groin, and focused on the road. She'd never let him drive again if he wrecked her car during his first turn behind the wheel. Hell, he'd probably never get another turn anyway. Daughters, especially immortal Daughters of Sigrid's era, liked to retain control of their surroundings, including a simple chore like driving.

"Why pizza?" she asked.

Her voice cut through his musings, dampening his growing desire. He cleared his throat and said, "Everybody likes pizza."

"What if I don't?"

He glanced across the car's interior. Her head was turned toward the passenger's side window, hiding most of her expression except the slight upturn of her mouth. "We can go somewhere else."

"Pizza's fine."

Then why had she asked? He shook his head and flicked on the turn signal, then eased into the turn lane for Highway 441 North behind two other vehicles. A Daughter's games. Was she going to be like that during their lunch date?

The arrow pointing left turned green and the cars in front of them accelerated into the turn. Will followed, half annoyed at himself. After waiting two years just to have her acknowledge him, he should be happy she'd asked him out, not nitpicking her behavior and wishing for more.

They chitchatted during the remainder of the drive to Franklin, mostly covering small town gossip. Tellowee wasn't that big, nor the People so numerous, that good news and bad could stay under wraps for long. Someone was always getting married or having a baby or fighting this scuffle or that. The familiarity of it all relaxed Will, easing the nervous energy plaguing him since that first kiss.

The parking lot next to Vito's was crowded when they turned into it off the Highlands Road. Will edged the Porsche into a parking space, then helped Sigrid out of the car, a courtesy she accepted with a regal tilt of her Scandinavian head.

They snagged the last free table in the packed room, scanned the menu, and agreed on toppings. As soon as the waitress took the order and hustled through crowded tables toward the kitchen, Sigrid fixed her cold blue eyes on him and said, "You are Anya Bloodletter's grandson."

Will sat back in his chair, unsurprised. Small town, small population. Everybody was related to everybody else in one way or another, and as a member of the Council of Seven, his grandmother was known by most.

"Yes," he said.

"She and I have waged many battles together."

His mouth curved into a faint smile. "I've heard some of the stories."

"Have you?" Sigrid's luscious mouth curved into a matching smile. "How long have you managed The Omega?"

"Unofficially? Since I was sixteen." Which was illegal in the state of Georgia or, at least, it was illegal to serve alcohol while under the legal age, but what the government didn't know wouldn't hurt anybody. "Mom and Dad started taking trips about then. Dad always wanted to travel, and with Casey growing up—"

"Casey?"

"My sister. Four years younger than me. You've probably seen her around the Omega."

Sig nodded, though whether she was acknowledging knowing Casey or merely agreeing with him, Will couldn't tell.

"Anyway." He shifted in his seat and ran his palms down his thighs, settling them there in a loose grip. "By the time I graduated from college and Casey started college, they were gone more often than they were home. It seemed kind of natural for them to hand over the reins to me."

"You enjoy bartending."

It wasn't a question. Will treated it as one anyway, unsure what else to say. "It can be fun watching the customers, giving people a safe and friendly place to go after work. What about you? How'd you get into genetics?"

Her faint smile turned rueful. "The calling found me. I had a knack for tending battlefield wounds, a skill most Daughters acquire over time if they value their hides."

Will grinned. Wasn't that the truth. Daughters, especially fighters like Sigrid, were always getting into scrapes. Sometimes those scrapes involved swords, guns, and other assorted weaponry, and the resulting wounds could be deadly, even for the immortals. Death claimed everybody, given enough time.

"Did you go to college?" he asked.

"I have," she acknowledged. "Several times, but not until arriving in the New World."

Will sat forward and braced his forearms on the tabletop. Her scent drifted over him, as it had when she'd visited his apartment that morning, and now as then, it stirred his senses from interest into desire.

He shook it off, disciplining himself, and focused on the conversation. "Where?"

"Harvard, first disguised as a man, later as myself, then Duke and Emory." She shrugged one shoulder, shifting the thin silk covering her upper body. It pulled against her breasts, highlighting them, and Will's mouth went dry. "I followed the early discoveries of DNA and its deciphering, and realized that if the People's underlying genetic structure could be untangled, we would gain a powerful tool in our quest to preserve our culture."

"So you became an expert."

"Yes." Her expression shifted infinitesimally, flashing momentarily into something less than happy, and cleared just as quickly. "Did you always want to tend bar?"

He shrugged. "I wanted to be a lot of things when I was a kid. Back in high school, I thought about going into genealogy, so when the career rotations came up in the ninth grade, I asked Dr. Upton if I could work with him."

"How long did you work in his office?"

"Still there," he said, and grinned. "Liked it so much, I started volunteering after the rotation was up. There's just something about digging into the past that gets under your skin. You must feel that a lot with the work you do."

Her eyelids lowered, covering the frigid blue of her irises. "The past is an ever present memory. I need not turn to work in order to feel it."

The poignancy underscoring her words pricked Will. He cupped a hand over hers, resting in her lap, and squeezed gently.

"Sorry."

Her eyes flashed up to his and widened. "Why?"

Because he should've known better than to bring up the past to a Daughter with as many battles under her belt as Sigrid had.

Just then, the owner appeared at the table carrying a piping hot pizza, and the mood was broken. Their conversation returned to the light banter they'd shared in the car and continued in that manner over the meal. When they were finished, Sigrid insisted on paying. Will barely refrained from rolling his eyes. He'd been taught better, and besides, Sons knew their places. By accepting Sigrid's invitation to lunch, he'd also accepted the role she wanted him to play.

For the moment, just until he could talk her into a more equitable arrangement.

He drove them back to the IECS compound more slowly than he'd driven to Franklin and parked in her allotted spot outside her office. She allowed him to help her out again, then stood in front of him with her hand in his and her head tilted to the side, studying him beneath lowered lashes.

That same old nervous energy enveloped him and he eased a fraction closer. She was right there, so close her breaths touched his skin, so close her mouth was a scant hand's breadth away.

She placed her free hand on his chest and ran a finger along the collar of his jacket. "Kiss me, Will Corbin, beloved Son of Wilhelmina the Fierce."

She didn't need to ask twice. He cupped her slender hips in his hands and urged her against him, meeting her halfway, and his mouth came down on hers in a gentle echo of their first two kisses. Soft, teasing, light. He flicked his tongue out, tasting her, and nearly groaned as her tongue touched his.

Sweet Mother. He'd wanted her so long, too long to stand in the middle of a public parking lot and neck with her without giving his desire away.

He ended the kiss abruptly, leaned his forehead against

hers, and pretended his chest wasn't heaving with every breath, that his dick wasn't half hard just from the simple touch of her mouth on his.

Her hand curled around his collar and tugged, and the corners of her mouth tilted up. "Tonight."

He tried to answer, cleared his throat of the desire choking him, and managed a hoarse, "Yeah?"

"I'll be at The Omega. Save a dance for me."

His hands tightened reflexively on her hips. A dance with Sigrid, the woman he'd wanted since the first time he laid eyes on her? Hell, yeah. He'd be there with bells on.

She leaned into him, brushed her lips against his again, then slipped away, her heels a sharp rap against the asphalt. Will stood there unable to turn around. One day he'd have to watch her walk away for good. When that time came, she'd leave him broken in ways he could only imagine. With an immortal Daughter, that was a given.

WILL LEFT his car parked where it was, in a guest spot outside Sigrid's office, and walked across the campus of the Institute for Early Cultural Studies, the People's leading research center. Here, top scientists worked on projects assigned by his cousin Rebecca Upton, the IECS's director, to further the People's ultimate goals: Cultural continuation, freedom from persecution, the fulfillment of the Prophecy of Light.

Every member, whether mortal or immortal, had a duty to aid the People. Most did, some didn't, but all kept those goals uppermost in their minds.

Will tapped a stray pebble with the toe of his dress shoe, then kicked it out of his path. The Omega played an important role in Tellowee, as similar places did in other communities where the People lived. It was a gathering spot, neutral territory where differences among families and individuals could be negotiated or ironed out. It also provided a safe haven for every patron to relax and enjoy herself for a few hours, without having to constantly look over her shoulder for coming danger.

Some, like Sigrid, always kept a sharp eye out. Habit or instinct, most likely, or a combination of both. A lax Daughter was a dead Daughter. Each learned that lesson early on, usually the hard way.

Sons were no different. Will jogged up the steps of the building housing Dr. Upton's office and pulled the outer door open. Male offspring were so rare, they were protected at all costs, including rigorous training in situational survival, martial arts, and the use of common weaponry, no different than their immortal sisters had when they were young.

Once training was completed, the difference in treatment between the two sexes could be stark. Daughters were cut loose and allowed freedoms that, until recently, had been forbidden to cosseted Sons. Only in modern times had Sons been allowed to choose their own mates, work outside the family, or travel on their own. The last hundred years or so of social innovation in the outside world had brought an echo of the same within the People.

Thank the Lady Ki he'd been born now and not back in the good ol' days when Daughters chained their men and kept them as virtual slaves.

Will stopped in front of Dr. Upton's office and frowned. It was locked tight, unusual for the time of day. Maybe Robert had had a late lunch or a doctor's appointment. Will shook his worry off, jotted a quick note, and pinned it to the bulletin board tacked to the wall outside the office. He checked his watch, sighed at the time, then backtracked to his truck. He'd drop by later on in the week, when he had more than a few minutes to spare.

The last of the late lunchers were trickling out of the Omega when Will parked in his reserved spot behind the bar. He slipped in through the employees' entrance carrying a change of clothes in his workout bag, then headed to his office, nodding polite greetings to the staff he passed.

If he focused, he could get through a chunk of the paperwork his accountant needed in order to file taxes for The Omega's previous business year.

As soon as he dropped into the chair behind his desk, Casey soared into his office looking like Armageddon was right around the corner. She slumped into a chair across the desk from him, rested her tray on her lap, and twisted her pretty mouth into a frown.

"I forbid it," she said.

He shuffled through the stack of files on his desk, searching for the printouts of last year's expenses. "Forbid what?"

"That woman."

He left off his search and leaned back in his chair. "Which woman would that be?"

"You know the one," Casey said, her voice a hair shy of a firm snap. "I forbid you from dating her."

Sigrid. Right.

Will shook his head. "Like you have a say."

"I'm the Daughter."

"You're a runt." One corner of his mouth curved upward. "How many times did it take you to pass basic firearms training? Four?"

"Three," she muttered, and scowled. "Why do you have to bring that up every time we argue?"

"Because every time we argue, it's over you trying to force me to do something I don't want to do."

"Mom would—"

Will jabbed a finger at her. "You aren't Mom."

"But I'm the—"

"And she and Dad are the only two people who might, maybe, in some small way, have a say in who I date."

Casey winced. "You're really going to date her?"

He stifled the impulse to retort, *her, who?* "We had lunch. She's dropping by tonight the way she always does. What are you worried about anyway? It's not like she's going to claim me or something."

Sigrid Glyvynsdatter could have any man she wanted without such formalities, more's the pity.

Casey's expression morphed into concern. "That's exactly what I'm worried about. I know how you feel about her."

"Casey, come on."

"No, Will, seriously. I know how you feel and I don't want you to get tangled up with her when she'll never feel the same way."

He barely hid his flinch. Trust Casey to hit the nail on the head. "I'll be fine."

"Sure."

"Really." He stood and walked around the desk, then knelt beside her, one hand on the back of her chair, the other on her knee. "I won't let things get out of hand. You know I won't."

"Maybe you won't be able to help yourself," she said in a tiny voice. "Maybe she'll smack some immortal Daughter mojo on you and you'll forget all your resolutions and I'll..."

"You'll what?" he asked gently.

"I'll lose the best brother I ever had."

"I'm the only brother you've ever had."

She cut a side-eyed smirk at him. "Yeah, so you're also the worst, but who's counting?"

He laughed and smacked a quick kiss to her cheek. "Go on. Get back to work."

"Can't keep the customers waiting," she muttered as she scooted off the chair and stood. "Especially those old as Eve Daughters."

"Smart ass," he said, and she grinned and blew a kiss to him, and flounced out the door looking much happier than when she'd entered.

Will dug into the paperwork with a light heart and slogged through as much as he could before the shift change. Five minutes before he was due in the bar proper, he slipped into the employees' bathroom and changed into his work clothes, a polo with the Omega's logo embroidered on the front, left-hand side, khakis, and tennis shoes.

Eric Reed, a mundane mortal who tended bar part-time, waved at Will as he stepped into the bar proper. "Hey, man. How's tricks?"

Will grinned and flipped open the bar's barrier. "Still doing. Busy lunch?"

Eric shrugged one muscled shoulder. "Good for a Monday in winter. Some new faces today."

Will grabbed a bar towel and bunched it up in his hands. "Yeah?"

"Yeah, you know." Eric shrugged again and his brown-gold gaze drifted across the sparse crowd dotting the room. "Young, hot women. Strong as ox men."

Will followed Eric's gaze to a table holding two women and a forty-something man, and a quartet of women ranging in age from late teens to matron sitting halfway across the room from the first group. Concern warred with curiosity. Tellowee got its share of People drifting through, but he usually knew most of them or was warned ahead of time. These faces were completely unfamiliar.

He snagged Eric's elbow and jerked his chin at the newcomers. "You mind hanging around a little longer? I need to go make nice."

A grin flashed across Eric's face, contrasting a white smile against his honey colored skin. "Sure, man. I can use the duckies."

Will tucked the towel into his back pocket and wound his way from behind the bar toward the first group. Their conversation halted as he drew near, and three sets of brown eyes focused on him, razor sharp. He stopped a few feet away and smiled. "Welcome to Tellowee. I'm Will Corbin, the Omega's manager."

The man stood, held out a calloused hand, and said in a guttural rumble, "Saul the Beguiler, grandson of Pari Bakhshesh.

This is my mother's sister, Chana Wolfbane, and her Daughter, Favi Soulbleeder."

Will clasped Saul's hand and shook it, measuring the other man as he was being measured in return. Saul was lean and tough. His dark eyes were hard flints in an expressionless face. Former military, probably. Most Sons were. If not for his parents' ownership of The Omega, Will would have given a career in the service serious consideration.

He let go of Saul's hand and nodded to his two companions. "If you don't mind my asking, what's your business here in Tellowee?"

Chana's tilted eyes regarded him solemnly over a pint of amber brew. "We hoped to renew a recent acquaintance. Jerusha Mankiller?"

Rebecca's youngest Daughter by birth and a good friend. Jerusha and her now-fiancé Drew Martin had returned from a trip to Turkey not long ago, bearing one set of the Bones of the Just.

Will looked the trio over again and made a snap decision. "My cousin. She lives about an hour from here. You want, I can call her for you, have her come up."

"Tell her to bring the hottie," Favi said in a soft, accented voice, and Chana's mouth quirked into a grin.

Will returned the grin with a saucy wink. "Sure thing. Help yourself to the menu. Today's on the house."

Saul's firm mouth twitched, not quite reaching a smile. "Thank you."

"Anytime. Let me know if you need anything."

Chana's smile turned secretive and her black eyelashes fluttered down, partially covering her beautiful eyes. "Oh, we will, sheereen-am."

Will left the table smiling and headed toward the other group of visitors, dismissing Chana's harmless flirtations as soon as he turned away.

Five

The afternoon's work was lightened by the midday repast's flirtations. Sigrid flew through the reports awaiting her attention, noting any anomalies, and sorted them by known hereditary family groups wherever possible. Soon, she and her team would be able to compile a genetic map from the Sisters through their children into the present day's populations.

Much work needed to be done before that could happen. Too many of those descendants had yet to return DNA samples to her office, in spite of the pressure placed on them by their heads of family. The piecemeal nature of the process could be frustrating, but it allowed work to be completed at a steady, methodical pace. Rushing through a backlog of tests would only lead to costly, time-consuming mistakes.

George knocked on her door an hour before the end of the work day, his young face set in a painfully apprehensive expression. "I'm leaving now. Doctor's appointment."

Sigrid pursed her lips, containing an exasperated sigh. "Why are you telling me?"

"In case you need anything before I go." He shifted from one foot to the other, and his gaze drifted away from hers. "Do you?"

"No," she said, her voice sharp. She released the sigh and tried again. George would never learn to face her as a man if she constantly rebuked him. "I'll see you tomorrow."

"Yeah, sure," he muttered, and shambled off with his shoulders hunched under the loose fabric of his sweater.

For a moment, something akin to concern pricked Sig's conscience. Was something wrong with the boy? He was never one for a snappy step, but lately he seemed even more languid than normal, and that hangdog air had become a permanent fixture.

She shook the concern off and focused on the screen of her desktop computer. If something was wrong, he would tell her, or she'd learn about it through the gossip that inevitably found her ear, whether she wanted it to or not.

At precisely five o'clock, Sigrid shut down her computer and tidied her desk. A quick trip home to change clothes and eat supper, and after, she could make good on her promise to meet Will at The Omega.

Anticipation curled through her. She placed a hand over her stomach, exactly where the odd feeling resided. Yes, anticipation, for a dance or another kiss, for the hope of Will's touch and attention. When last had a man aroused even that emotion within her?

Her eyelids slid closed as memory failed. Too long without then, so long she'd forgotten what the first, heady glory of having a man catch her interest felt like.

It wouldn't do to appear overeager and risk having Will take her attention for granted.

And because of that, she slowed her pace and took her time driving home, picking out appropriate clothing, and eating supper. More than two hours later, she parked her Porsche in the Omega's oddly crowded parking lot and entered, automatically assessing the knots of patrons scattered around the room. She noted the locations of those faces she was unfamiliar with, nodded to a few she knew, and caught a flash of long, black hair out of the corner of her eye.

The glimpse was fleeting, barely long enough for recognition to strike. Sigrid frowned. Min Li Snow Dragon. Moira wouldn't be happy to see that Daughter again so soon after Min Li had delayed Moira while Tom was kidnapped.

A low, husky laugh snagged Sigrid's attention, and she turned toward the bar. Will was leaning against it flirting with a Daughter, his smile too familiar for Sigrid's taste. Was this the woman Moira had warned her about, the one who held Will's heart? If so, why had he kissed Sig, accepted a date, and laughed and flirted with her? Why did he not pursue this paragon rather than spending his time with a woman he could never love?

The anticipation of seeing him withered into a tiny knot in her chest. And because he had, because he'd accepted Sigrid's attention in this woman's stead, was the other woman not too late? Now that Sigrid had singled him out, this upstart would simply have to find another man to dig her hooks into until Sigrid had decided exactly what she was going to do with Will Corbin.

Resolution firmed, she walked half a dozen steps in his direction, intending to set the smiling couple straight before flirtation developed into a liaison. A redheaded spitfire stepped into her path and held a hand up, halting Sigrid halfway to her destination.

"Hold yer ever lovin' horses there, Sig," Moira said. "Where do ye think ye're off to?"

Sigrid jerked her chin at the bar. "Will and I arranged a dance this evening. I've come to claim it."

"Ye'll do no such thing. Young Will there deserves a bit of happiness."

Irritation lifted Sigrid's chin. "And he won't find it with me?"

"No, he won't," Moira shot back. "All ye're after is another notch in that hunk of iron ye call a sword."

The blow hit too close to the mark. Sigrid stared down her nose at the smaller Daughter and curled her upper lip into a deliberate sneer. "What if I am? I'll take care of him when I'm through."

"Take care! Is that what ye call dumping the boy and breaking his heart?"

"You said he was in love with another woman," Sigrid said stiffly. "Therefore, his heart won't be involved in the least."

Moira's gritty resolve melted into a pitying expression. "Ye've done enough damage here, Sig. Let the lad be, or ye'll have me to contend with, and all me kin, too."

Sigrid huffed out a short laugh. "We've never quarreled over men before."

"This one is worth the bother. Have ye told his gran of yer interest?"

"Anya Bloodletter is an old friend."

"Aye, she is at that, but have ye told her?"

Sigrid kept her expression carefully blank. "Not yet."

Moira narrowed her pale blue eyes into shrewd slits. "Ye're afraid she'll see right through ye and reject yer claim."

"I fear no Daughter," Sigrid said, her voice icy.

"On a battlefield, aye, ye're the equal of most," Moira agreed calmly, "but where the heart's concerned, ye've always held fear. How many husbands have ye claimed?"

Sigrid snapped her jaws shut. Never had she taken a husband, only ever lovers, and Moira well knew that to be so. "What's your point?"

"Young Will deserves a bit of happiness," Moira repeated. "He'll no' find it in your less than tender care, will he?"

Sigrid glanced toward Will. His hands were busy polishing glasses, but his gaze rested on the unknown Daughter. It was soft, kind, and held a tender note she'd never seen him direct her way. "What's the Daughter's name?"

Moira turned and her gaze followed Sigrid's to Will. "Chana Wolfbane."

"I know of her," Sigrid murmured. "She's a good Daughter. Strong."

"That she is."

"You're willing to risk our friendship over a man?"

"Over this one, aye." Moira faced Sigrid and clapped a hand to Sigrid's arm. "Be a shame to muss yer chiseled cheekbones with a blow of me fist."

Sigrid reluctantly pulled her attention away from Will and mustered a knowing smile for her friend. "And risk the babe's health?"

"Oh, the babe will have a hand in the blow, too." Moira jerked her chin at the entrance. "Go on home with ye, now. Have a proper think on the matter without yer loins turning ye cross-eyed."

"As if," Sigrid huffed. "I'll be back to watch the next ACC game."

"I'm counting on it."

Sigrid pivoted and left without looking back, but above the crowd's lively chatter, a low male laugh drifted to her, teasing her with what could be.

WILL WOKE slowly the next morning, his mind clouded with the night's dreams. Sigrid leaning against him, laughing up into his face, her hands stroking his chest. Sigrid kissing him, her passion as great as his own.

Sigrid backing away from him, her ice blue eyes frozen and unfeeling.

He raked a hand over his face, tucked it behind his head, and blinked up at the ceiling. He'd waited for her all night, searched the face of every person entering The Omega, and not once had it been her. The tiny disappointments mounted up over the evening until eventually, they grew into a huge lump lodged in his throat.

She'd broken her promise, something no Daughter did without due consideration. He should've known he wouldn't hold her attention for long.

"Goddamn it," he muttered, and yanked the covers off his legs, baring them to the room's chill. He rolled out of bed, inched the heat up to a respectable temperature, and slogged into the bathroom under the heavy weight of resignation.

Blessed Mother, why had he allowed himself to hope for even one second?

He drowned the faint hurt clinging to him under a hot shower, attempted to scrub it away, and finally, when the water was too cold to tolerate, he turned it off and got dressed for the day.

His cellphone was blinking when he retrieved it from the bedside nightstand. He opened the notifications, thumbed into his messages, and grunted. Rebecca wanted him to drop by her office as soon as he could, today if possible. He stuck his cellphone in his back pocket and finished getting ready. Food could wait, and probably should, given the hopeless ache knotted in his stomach.

By the Lady Ki, he had it bad.

Half an hour later, he jogged up the steps of the IECS's main administrative building toward Rebecca's office and checked in with her secretary, then plopped onto the couch in the waiting area and thumbed through the current issue of *World of the People.*

Six pages in, a picture of a Greek cup depicting an Amazon warrior on horseback was printed opposite a short paragraph speculating that the Bones of the Just had been found. Will shook his head. That wasn't quite true. Only three sets had been found, as far as he knew, but even those few were cause for celebration.

Rebecca opened her office door before he could finish reading the article and held her hands out to him. "Will, darling, thank you for stopping by on such short notice."

He dropped the magazine onto the coffee table, surreptitiously eyeing his cousin as he stood. Dark circles colored the once-smooth skin under her eyes, now marred by fine lines, and her normally rigid posture wasn't quite stick straight. In spite of that, her red business suit was pressed and neat, her fine blonde hair was tucked perfectly into place, and her hands were steady, as only a warrior's of her experience could be.

He crossed the room and pecked a kiss to her cheek, and breathed in the faintest hint of jasmine perfume. "You look tired."

Her laughter was soft and not quite full. "Work has consumed too much of my attention of late."

"So Robert's ok?"

A flash of concern flitted across her expression and was just as quickly tucked away. "As well as can be expected."

"I dropped by his office yesterday afternoon."

"Oh." She waved a hand and stepped back, inviting him into her office. "He stayed home yesterday. Said he hasn't been sleeping well."

"Neither have you," he said, and closed the doors behind himself. "What's really going on?"

"Work," she said firmly. "Can I get you something to drink? Some water, perhaps?"

He shook his head, but let her evasiveness go. "I'm fine. You said you wanted to talk to me?"

"Yes, dear. Have a seat." She sank onto a settee situated on one side of the room and held a hand out to the chair beside it. "We have some new faces in town."

Will sat and hooked one ankle across the opposite knee. "Yeah. A couple of different groups came in yesterday."

"They're likely the first of many. Word has gotten out. The Oracle has awakened. The Bones of the Just are being located, when they were lost for millennia." She shrugged and clasped her hands in her lap. "Some believe the Prophecy of Light is on the verge of being fulfilled."

Excitement gripped Will, crowding out the despondency of Sigrid's rejection. "Holy shit."

Rebecca laughed and relaxed into the settee. "Indeed."

"Sorry," he muttered. "It's just, the Prophecy of Light was a myth until Maya and James translated it."

"And yet, one by one its components are coming true." She leaned forward and brushed her fingertips over his knee, her laughter lost to an earnest expression. "Tellowee could be the gathering place spoken of in the Prophecy."

"The Bones of the Just," he murmured. Three sets found, four more to go, and the Sisters' remains would finally be gathered together in one place for the first time in who knew how long. "What do you want me to do?"

A sly smile lifted the corners of Rebecca's mouth. "How do you know I want something?"

"You asked for a meeting."

"Age has dulled my subtlety. I'm sorry, darling."

He clasped her fingers in his and smiled. "Anything you need, I'm here. You know that."

"And that's exactly why I called you, that and because of The Omega."

"The natural spot for newcomers to go."

"Making you the perfect person to handle those newcomers." She exhaled slowly and tightened her grip on his fingers. "I knew I could count on you to grasp the situation quickly. The influx of members of the People is likely to be slow for a while, but soon, it could overrun our ability to house and feed everyone. I need someone to coordinate our efforts, to secure safe housing and supplies."

"You're not talking about food," he said slowly.

"There's something coming, Will, something..." She sucked in a breath and visibly gathered her composure. "We must be prepared for every eventuality."

"I'll take care of it."

"I know, darling. Thank you." She squeezed his fingers a final time and released his hand, then sat back and speared him with the regard of the battlefield commander she'd been for so long. "Now, we have food, weapons, and ammunition stored in the caves behind the IECS, in the oldest parts of the Archives."

Will took out his cellphone and opened up the memo app,

and jotted down the names of the people in charge of the IECS's stores. In the back of his mind, worry lingered. Rebecca was holding back on him, hiding something important. He'd figure it out eventually, but in the meantime, it looked like his workload had just doubled, and at a time when he most needed the distraction.

Six

Sigrid settled into her desk with a fresh batch of test results. Now that the entire staff was up to speed on testing procedures, the backlog of DNA waiting to be tested was rapidly diminishing. Soon, new samples would be tested upon arrival, and once that happened, she could begin selecting a team to sort through the results and collate them with genealogical records. Any changes in the mitochondrial DNA of the family groups could then be tracked, and if luck held, the specific remains of the Sisters could be identified, by process of elimination if nothing else.

Such a hope stretched luck to the limit and beyond, true, but it was better to prepare for the best outcome along with the worst.

It had been three days since her lunch with Will.

Sigrid closed the report she was working on, a completed test for an immortal Daughter whose origins were well documented, and selected another report. Moira had been right. A few days apart from the dashing young bartender had helped clear Sigrid's head. She still hadn't decided what to do about him in the long run, but her desire for him had refused to wane since their last meeting.

Experience was a good teacher. Most men who captured her interest held it only briefly, not even long enough for a good fuck.

Will wasn't most men. His initiative in claiming a kiss intrigued her. Coupled with his strong will and excellent bloodlines, his boldness had piqued her interest.

She'd give it a few more days before making a final decision. There was no hurry. She wasn't going anywhere in the near future, and neither was he.

Unless the woman he wanted turned up.

A faint knot clenched Sigrid's stomach. She frowned and touched her fingers to the unusual feeling gripping her. A stomach bug, no doubt. Immortal Daughters weren't completely unsusceptible to illness, but it was so rare as to be a myth.

Imagine, a fierce warrior descended from generations of Daughters falling prey to the flu. Such a laughable fancy.

Sigrid shook her head and resumed her study of the report in front of her, supplanting her thoughts of Will and a possible illness. George had been instrumental in training the new staff. He was a brilliant geneticist and, in spite of his unfortunate tendency toward softness, was quite good at integrating the staff into a cohesive, efficient workforce.

A soft knock sounded on her office door. Her heart thumped erratically in her chest. *Will.* But no, of course it wouldn't be him. Will hadn't once tried to contact her since their lunch date.

Had he already forgotten the kisses he'd stolen, and the one she'd freely given?

One corner of her mouth turned down. Why was she so worried about that?

The door opened and George stuck his head inside, forestalling her thoughts from spiraling out of control. "Do you have a minute, Dr. Glyvynsdatter?"

Sigrid pushed away from her desk and stood. "Of course, Mr. Howe. What is it?"

"We had a mix-up in the lab. Two samples." He edged all the way inside and held up two file folders, one in each hand. "I need permission to request retests."

"You have the forms ready, I presume."

"Sure. Ah." He stepped forward and handed the folders to her. "You're not mad?"

She arched an eyebrow. "Why would I be?"

"Well, you know. Ah." He huffed out a breath and his cheeks flushed pink. "We goofed."

"It wouldn't be the first time a human has erred."

"Oh. Right. Sorry."

"Stop apologizing for wrongs you haven't committed," she said mildly, then bent her head to the folders. A moment later, the requisite permission forms were signed, clearing the way for him to draft formal letters requesting new samples. "There. I expect this to be taken care of as soon as possible."

"Yes, Dr. Glyvynsdatter."

She sat down, automatically dismissing him, and returned to her own work.

George shuffled his feet.

Sigrid stifled her first response, an irrational irritation, and glanced up. "Is something wrong?"

He opened his mouth, closed it, and sighed. "No, ma'am. I'll get right on this."

"See that you do."

His shoulders slumped a fraction, but he turned around and left without saying another word. She stared after him as the knot in her stomach tightened. His clothes were veritably hanging off the poor boy's frame. Had he lost weight recently? She pulled his form up in her memory, the long, nearly flawless memory of an immortal Daughter. When he'd first come to the IECS, George had been quite a bit heftier, and had stayed that way until just a few weeks ago. Was his weight loss deliberate then, or was something truly wrong?

She dismissed the thought as soon as it occurred. If something were wrong, George would tell her. She was his boss, after all, and the Daughter responsible for his welfare. It was his duty to immediately report to her any harm that had befallen him. He was a sensible young man, if a bit tender yet, and had never failed in his duty. There was absolutely no reason to worry over him.

This stomach bug, on the other hand, could be quite the nuisance. Twice in one day, it had plagued her. First thing next week, she'd call Dr. Phillips and schedule a checkup.

Mind settled, she returned to her work, the men in her life all but forgotten.

BY FRIDAY, Will had almost talked himself into believing Sigrid had lost her interest in him. He ignored the stab to his heart and, if he were honest, his ego as he sliced lemons ahead of the weekend crowd's thirst. So what if his chance had been fleeting at best? At least he'd gotten a chance. It was more than he'd ever expected.

The Omega's front doors opened and in walked Chana Wolfbane wearing a richly decorated, blue jacket over a matching shirt and loose, flowing pants. Her dark hair was held away from her face by strings of metal and hung down her back in long ringlets, and the hilt of a sword peeked over her right shoulder.

She smiled at him across the nearly empty bar and headed straight for him, followed by her daughter and nephew. Favi and Saul peeled off halfway across the hardwood floor and snagged an empty table.

Will mustered a smile for Chana as she approached. "You look nice."

"Thank you." Her skin shone under the lighting hung over the bar proper as she tilted her head in a coy nod. "We will be eating here tonight. Do you have a menu?"

"I'll have Casey bring one to your table." He dropped the paring knife in the sink, covered the lemons, and slid them into the mini-fridge under the bar. "You know, there are a lot nicer places to eat in this area. I can get you a list."

Which reminded him. He needed to update that list and

make more copies for the influx of visitors Rebecca had warned him to expect. That would come in handy sooner or later. Maybe he should make a welcome packet or something.

"We enjoy eating here." Chana placed her slim hands on the bar's edge, and her eyelashes fluttered down, covering her nearly black eyes. "Dancing is a custom among the People here? To dance with someone who interests you?"

Will nodded and leaned against the bar across from her. "Sure. It's one of the more polite ways of courting."

"Then we shall dance later, yes?"

Her request caught him off guard. Chana was, like many Daughters, a beautiful woman, athletic, intelligent, and eternally young, or nearly so. He'd been so caught up in Sigrid, he'd completely missed seeing Chana as anything but another customer to be cajoled, served, or satisfied, whatever the occasion called for. Now, he eyed her the way a man would an attractive woman, searching for an emotion, any emotion. His heart was rock steady, no desire flooded him the way it did with Sigrid, but Chana was still a desirable woman with an impeccable pedigree.

He could do a lot worse.

And what harm would it do to share a dance with her? He needed a distraction right now, anything to get his mind off of Sigrid. A light flirt with Chana might be just the ticket.

Chana's eyes narrowed, so slightly only someone standing next to her would notice. "You have another?"

The question shot right into his heart, awakening a sharp regret. He pushed it down and shook his head. "I'd love to dance with you."

Her expression relaxed into an answering smile. "When you are free."

"Of course." He hesitated a minute, then clasped a hand over hers and squeezed lightly. In for a penny, in for a pound. "I'll come by your table later."

She flipped her hand over in his and met him palm to palm. The friction warmed his skin, and did not a blessed thing to stir his interest.

Oh, well. Sigrid had always been the only woman to move him on sight anyway. Maybe he just needed time to shake her memory off before he tried being with another woman.

Chana slipped away and walked toward her family, just as Casey stepped up to him at the bar. His sister jerked her chin at the other Daughter. "Who's that?"

"Chana Wolfbane. She's new here. Long story."

On the other hand, he might need Casey's help soon, depending on how right Rebecca was about upcoming events. His hands were already full, between managing the bar, volunteering with Robert, and the few days he'd put into familiarizing himself with the IECS's supplies. He hadn't even started contacting locals yet to see where any possible overflow of visitors could be housed. An extra set of hands on this would be a godsend.

Briefly, he outlined his newly assigned duties and tacked on an overview of why Rebecca had asked him to help out.

When he was finished, Casey leveled a neutral gaze on him. "That doesn't explain why that Daughter was holding your hand."

Will glanced away, hiding the hurt that popped up every time he thought about Sigrid. "It's nothing. Just a dance."

"Just a dance, huh." Casey sighed, then stood on her tiptoes and pressed a soft kiss to his cheek. "Well if this *just a dance* gets out of hand, let me know and I'll help you handle her."

He snorted out a laugh. "In your dreams, creampuff."

"Ooo. Just you wait 'til Mom gets back," she gritted out, and he swung her up into a bear hug right there behind the bar and peppered sloppy kisses all over her face until she managed to wiggle out of his arms, protesting the whole time.

Will's mood improved after that, and stayed exactly where he liked it through the first rush of after work customers and the bigger rush of an after supper bunch. Moira and Tom came in not long after and worked their way through the growing crowd, him toward his usual table where the other Professorteers sat, and her toward the bar.

Will poured her a cold cup of filtered water, added a slice of lime to the rim, and set it on the bar in front of her as she approached.

"What's this?" she asked.

"Water."

Her delicate features twisted into a grimace. "Feckin' water. What're ye doing, treating me like a tot?"

"You'll get water until the baby's here," he said, and forestalled her next comment with a firm, "I don't care if beer is mother's milk in Ireland."

A grin broke through her grimace. "Aye, ye're quick on the uptake there, boy-o."

"I have to be around you," he retorted, and hustled off to help another customer.

Around nine, some poor sap slid a quarter into the jukebox and keyed in a slow love song. The first few measures cut through the noise of chatter and laughter and clinking glasses, subduing it, and whoever was nearest the main light switch dimmed it, right on cue. Will glanced through the throng of people streaming on and off the dance floor, searching for Chana, and spotted her playing pool with Favi, Maya Bellegarde, and another Daughter whose back was turned to him.

He filled an order, set it on the bar, and just as he was thinking of taking a break to dance with Chana, the doors opened on Sigrid.

His heart stuttered to a stop in his chest, and he cursed it under his breath. Damn it. When would he ever learn?

She sauntered toward him, slicing through the crowd like it didn't exist as he built a lager for her. He set it down in front of her just as she settled against the bar.

"Hello," she said, and her lips tilted into a soft smile.

Moira took one look at Sigrid, shot the other Daughter a sour glance, and pivoted away from the bar, marching as if the very devil were on her heels.

Will attempted a welcoming smile for Sigrid, and when his mouth refused to cooperate, settled for a stiff nod. "Let me know if you need anything."

Her smile deepened. "As a matter of fact, I do. I came to claim a dance."

A laugh huffed out of him before he could stop it. "Right. Well, I'm busy tonight."

"Not too busy for me."

Her matter of fact tone pricked him harder than it should've. He leaned toward her across the bar and lowered his voice, for the sake of propriety if not her sensibilities, or his own hide. Daughters tended to swing first and ask questions later at the first hint of an insult thrown their way, whether one was intended or not.

"Sorry, sweetheart," he said. "Somebody else beat you to the punch."

He let that sink in for a minute, waited for her to react. Her smile slid off her face and was replaced by the careful scrutiny of a scientist regarding an unusual specimen, nothing more, nothing less. No matter how hard he searched, he found not one sign of interest or temper in her expression, not one Mother blessed sign that Sigrid had a problem with him dancing with another woman.

He rocked back on his heels and tried not to let her indifference hurt, yet there it was, throbbing in his heart like it always did.

Fuck it. If she didn't want him, another woman would.

He nodded as politely as he could, then turned away in search of someone to fill his spot at the bar. A deal was a deal. Chana would get her dance, and if she wanted more, he'd do his damnedest to figure out how to give it to her.

SIGRID SIPPED her lager as she turned her back to the bar and scanned the people on the dance floor. It had taken all her discipline to keep her expression under control during her conversation with Will.

So, the woman he had his eye on had come around, and at one of the worst times possible.

Instinct warred within her, pushing her in opposite directions. Fight for the boy, leave him to the other woman. This was why Daughters were better off taking lovers they could never be personally interested in.

Not that she was personally interested in this one, but still. He'd captured her attention and was an attractive man. In a few years, once the People's current troubles were over, he would've made a good father.

The lager slid down her throat, cool and heady, and she savored its yeasty bite as she sorted through each aspect of the situation. The match would cement her longstanding friendship with Anya Bloodletter, something neither had achieved in the many centuries since they'd first met, but such a match could only be made if Anya agreed to Sigrid's suit. With another Daughter in the picture, one Will apparently admired and possibly held feelings for, Sigrid's own claim might be subsumed by the interests of his heart.

As if love were the most important factor in a match involving a beloved Son.

Sigrid took another sip and cupped the mug between her palms. It wasn't disappointment unfurling within her. It was the loss of a strategic connection within the People, nothing more.

Will reappeared at the edge of the dance floor, leading a familiar Daughter into the crowded space. Sigrid searched her memory and immediately landed on the woman he'd been flirting with just a few nights past, when Moira had issued her warning.

But that Daughter was new to Tellowee. Could she and Will have been engaging in a long distance relationship while the Daughter handled business elsewhere?

The question spooled out in Sigrid's mind, occupying a large chunk of her attention during the song playing over the speakers. She watched Will and the woman dance, watched him bend his head toward her and whisper humor into her ear, watched the woman flirt and charm as her hands subtly explored Will's chest and arms.

Sigrid's stomach curled into a knot, surprising her. Maybe the lager had aggravated whatever bug she'd picked up. She set it aside and resumed her observations, and when the song ended and Will led the other Daughter off the dance floor, she found herself at its edge, directly in their path.

Will stopped abruptly some three feet in front of Sigrid. "Yes?"

"I wish a dance." The words came out softer than she'd meant, less determined and more questioning. She cleared her throat, straightened her spine, and stared down her nose at him. "Now."

The Daughter skirted Will and stopped at his side, her hand held within his larger one. She was a pretty woman, willowy compared to Sigrid's solid Nordic build, and delicately clad in a hand embroidered silk jacket over more practical wear.

Sigrid swallowed down the automatic dislike and nodded. "Sigrid Deathknell, daughter of Glyvyn the Ice Warrior, of the line of Bagda."

The woman nodded in return, her dark gaze expressionless. "Chana Wolfbane, daughter of Pari Bakhshesh, of the line of Eleni."

"Well met, kaetyrm."

"And you." Chana's hand tightened on Will's and she peeked at him out of the corners of her luminous eyes. "Thank you, Will. I'll see you tomorrow."

Will smiled down at her, his expression open and kind. "Of course. Be safe."

Chana bowed to Sigrid, then eased into the crowd, leaving them alone, if anyone could be alone in a room filled with people.

Sigrid deliberately reached out to Will and clasped the hand

Chana had not held. "Shall we?"

Will gazed at her for a long moment, his green eyes shuttered above the hard set of his sensuous mouth. A strange sensation fluttered in Sigrid's stomach. He was going to refuse. She'd waited too long, and now his woman was here, come to love him. Why had she listened to Moira? Why had she hesitated to press her claim?

At last, Will twined his fingers with hers and tugged, pulling her into his arms as he stepped onto the dance floor. He held her close, closer than he'd held Chana, and brushed his cheek against hers.

She relaxed against him, allowing the music to sweep over her, and swayed to its beat against Will's warmth.

His hands slid from her waist around her back, holding her firmly. "I missed you."

"Hmm." She sighed into his throat, inhaled, and caught a hint of cologne mingling with the faint hint of sharply scented soap. "I missed this."

"Dancing?" He huffed out a laugh, ruffling her hair, and rubbed one hand across the low of her back. "Where were you?"

"Busy."

"So busy you had to break your word to me?"

She stiffened, tried to draw back, and was held exactly where she was, tightly pressed against him. "I never break my word."

"You were supposed to be here days ago."

"I was busy," she said, enunciating each word.

"And you're not going to tell me what you were doing?"

"I owe you no such explanation."

He stilled and eased away from her. One hand slid up her back and cupped her nape under her braid, pinning her as surely as he had when he'd led her onto the dance floor. "Do you want me?"

She arched one eyebrow. "Have I not made that clear?"

"No, you haven't. Look." His hand squeezed her nape, gentle for all his strength. "No games, ok? If you can't play it

straight with me, if you can't be here when you say you will, then
it's a no go. I'm not going to let you toy with me."

"I'm not—"

His mouth came down on hers, silencing her words, and she
opened for him without meaning to, opened and softened and
met him kiss for kiss as her fingers twisted into his shirt and his
hands tangled in her hair. Her heart rocketed in her chest, racing
so fast, she could scarcely catch her breath, and still, Will kissed
her, touched her, gentled her.

His fingers dug into her skin for one brief moment, then he
drew back and touched his forehead to hers. A solid erection
pressed into her lower stomach, just above the juncture of her
thighs, and his breath shuddered out of him with every beat of his
heart against hers.

"Never lie to me," he said. "Not ever."

She nodded mutely, too overwhelmed by their shared
passion to deny him.

They danced to the end of the song, holding each other at a
sedate distance, belying the desire racing through Sigrid's blood.
His kiss, that beautiful, achingly real kiss. She didn't know what
to make of it, couldn't think around the heat ricocheting within
her, and so when the song ended and another took its place, she
allowed him to lead her back to the bar, accepted the fresh lager
he built for her, and spent the rest of the evening observing the
man who'd stolen her reason with the intensity of one kiss.

Seven

The dance with Sigrid lingered in Will's mind the rest of Friday and well into his dreams that night. Saturday morning, he awoke restless, edgy, and so hard, he could barely walk.

It was ridiculous how easily she aroused him.

As soon as he rolled out of bed, he texted Ethan Phillips, the People's local doctor and a cousin on Will's mother's side, and arranged to meet the other Son in midmorning at the gym in Clayton. Sex was off the menu. Lifting weights wasn't the best substitute, but it was better than nothing.

During the drive into the nearby town, Will's thoughts inevitably turned to Sigrid. She'd been beautiful last night, radiant, like a goddess risen from the North Atlantic, cold and deadly and fierce.

Until that kiss.

Desire flickered through him, and he shifted in the seat of his truck, spreading his knees wide to accommodate his burgeoning erection. Sweet Mother, she'd felt so good rubbing up against him with her hands on his chest and her mouth so giving under his. Another kiss like that, and he might drag her into his office and take her whether they were both ready or not.

He wasn't.

The lone car ahead of him slowed as it approached a steep

curve near the local public library. Will eased off the gas and applied the brake automatically, his thoughts tangled in a knot over Sigrid.

Did she want him or not? And if she did, was he really prepared for what that entailed? Two years of wanting her might not be enough when push came to shove. Or maybe it would weaken him to her, breaking him when he most needed to stand firm, and in the doing, he would lose her.

Ahead, the other car's left turn signal blinked on, and it turned onto the back street leading to downtown. Will waited for it to clear the lane, then matched his truck's speed to the posted limit as he drove past the library and the civic center into downtown Clayton.

She enjoyed his kisses, that was pretty damn clear, and she claimed to want him. Why else would she take the time to track down his name and address, take him to lunch, and make a point of dancing with him?

Then again, why had she broken her promise to meet him earlier in the week? If it was all a game to her, why had she bothered to come back to The Omega? True, it was the only nightlife in Tellowee and a lot of the local People gathered there, but there were other options if she really needed to get out. Clayton wasn't that far away and it had its fair share of restaurants and live music, especially in the summer. The music scene was slower now that true winter had arrived, but not that slow. There were still plenty of outsiders wandering through to keep things interesting.

Will huffed out a sigh, negotiated the last few turns into the gym's parking lot, and parked. It was pointless to dwell on a Daughter's reasons for doing anything. Sigrid would tell him what was going on or not, and nothing he said or did would change her mind either way. So far, the only thing that worked on her was kissing her into silence.

Oddly enough, he was ok with that.

A sleek, black Tesla Model S pulled up beside Will's truck.

He snagged his gym bag, slid out of his truck, and grinned at Ethan over the top of the other Son's car. "Snazzy ride."

Ethan laughed and slammed his car door shut. "You're just aiming for a turn behind the wheel."

"Absolutely."

They met on the sidewalk and walked in together, a sharp contrast in looks, if not in build. Ethan was maybe two inches taller than Will and had darker skin and auburn hair, though they both shared the light green eyes that seemed to pop up in random intervals in their line of the family, no doubt inherited from some captured mate. It wasn't unusual for Daughters to kidnap men with uncommon traits and breed with them, hoping to improve their offspring's chances of surviving in a world that too often sought to destroy them.

The gym was packed with men and women of all ages and shapes. Will nodded at two Daughters he knew more by sight than anything, then he and Ethan headed toward the men's locker room, ignoring the gazes of the mortal women tracking their progress.

They'd worked out together enough to understand each other's routines. By unspoken consent, they headed for the free weights, eschewing the machines, and settled into a steady, upper body workout. No competitive muscle flexing, no adversarial remarks, just the nice, relaxing burn of man versus iron.

During a lull between biceps curls and bench presses, Ethan rubbed a towel over his face, drying off the sweat, and leveled a speculative gaze on Will. "So tell me, cuz. How does a Son handle two Daughters in one night?"

Will's heart thumped once. He snagged his bottle of water and hid his nerves behind a long, slow sip. Friggin' grapevine. Nobody could get away with anything in Tellowee without rumor spreading like wildfire.

He set the water aside, then adjusted the weights for the next set of reps. "If you came by The Omega more often, you'd figure that one out for yourself."

Ethan shot Will a wicked grin, flashing even, white teeth. "I don't have to stoop to bar crawling to get my women."

"Yet somehow you managed to lose Serafina Noland to Levi Ewart."

Ethan's grin morphed into a sour scowl. "Low blow, man."

"All's fair in love and war." Will jerked his chin at the weights. "Are we going to work out or what?"

"Work out." Ethan laid down on the bench, curled his hands around the bar above him, and adjusted his position relative to it. "You've never been much for talking about women, but this evasiveness is bad, even for you."

Will settled at the head of the bench, in the spotter's position. "Stop psychoanalyzing me, Doc."

"I mean it."

"I danced with two women in one night. Any other time you'd be congratulating me."

"Any other time, I wouldn't worry about your being in the middle of an epic catfight." Ethan lifted the weighted bar off its supports and lowered it slowly to his chest. His breath hissed out steadily as he raised it high again. "Speaking of catfights, it's been a while since we've had an exhibition."

"School has one every month."

"For the kids, yeah. What about for us? Grown men need to vent their aggression on a regular basis."

Will grinned down at his cousin. "Is that your way of saying you want to have a go at Levi for stealing Serafina away from you?"

Ethan's muttered curse ended in a huff as he finished his first set. "Just set one up. It'll take all our minds off what's going on."

"Yeah, and help settle the restless natives, too."

Will and Ethan exchanged positions. Will worked through half his reps, then said, "How's the hospital doing on medical supplies?"

Ethan arched an eyebrow at Will. "I hadn't planned on

drawing blood when I dragged Levi onto the mat."

Since Levi had just married his pretty little mortal, there was a good chance Ethan would be the one bleeding at the end of any fight between the two men, sanctioned or not.

Will shrugged off the possibilities, finished his reps, and set the bar back in its support. Ethan could take care of himself, the same as any Son, though most shied away from pursuing another Son's woman. Nobody wanted a war with another family, especially when that other family included a Daughter like Hawthorne the Beheader, a newly appointed member of the Council of Seven. Will's grandmother would feel duty bound to intercede on behalf of her long dead sister, Ethan's ancestress. Since Anya was also a member of the People's ruling body, the rift between her and Hawthorne could tear the People apart, just when they most needed to unite.

Will sat up and shook the faint muscle burn out of his arms. "We've got a lot of new faces in town."

"Including one of the Daughters you danced with." At Will's even glance, Ethan shrugged. "Small town."

"Yeah, well, we're liable to get a huge influx of new faces into that small town over the next few weeks."

"Rebecca's been talking to you, too, huh?"

"Yeah. So, about those medical supplies."

"We're working on it."

"Let me know if you need help stocking up or finding a place to store stuff. I may want you to go over the supplies stored at the Archives, too, and you might want to think about stocking up on blood, if you can."

Ethan stilled, his expression suddenly serious. "It's that bad?"

"Maybe, maybe not." Though in his gut, Will was beginning to feel the storm gathering around them. "Never hurts to be prepared."

"I'll second that."

They finished their workout and arranged to meet early

Monday afternoon for a game of one on one at the Rec Department's gym in Tiger, south of Clayton. Will wiggled a promise out of Ethan to drop by The Omega that night, then he headed home and got ready for work, his body loose, his mind clearer than when he'd first awoken.

THE MORNING after her dance with Will, Sigrid rose well before her usual waking time and grumbled into a steaming hot cup of coffee. What had gotten into her of late? He was just a man, like the many she'd had before, no more or less important than any other, and that's exactly what had kept her sane through her centuries-long life.

He'd seemed reluctant.

She sighed and rubbed gritty eyes with her fingers, then plodded into her bathroom and set her coffee mug on the counter next to the sink. The problem here wasn't Will. It was her strategy. Obviously the few days she'd needed to sort through her own intentions had driven a small wedge between them and cooled his ardor. That was in the past now and couldn't be helped, but doubt remained in her mind over which path to take. Push him to accede to her demands, or give him time to grow accustomed to her?

So many doubts, where none had ever before dwelt.

She shook them off, twisted her hair into a knot. An itchy restlessness remained, crawling under her skin. It was almost as if she were girding for battle. That's what the feeling reminded her of, only in this instance, the stakes weren't her death or Will's, but their possible future.

It sounded so permanent when she thought of it in that manner.

Work. That would distract her from these useless ruminations. Focusing on another task, an important one, would give her the distance she needed to cultivate a clear, objective view of the situation with Will. It was Saturday, true, and he expected her at The Omega later that evening, but until then, she needed to burn off the restless energy plaguing her.

A workout first, then work, and later, another dance.

Schedule settled, she slipped on workout clothes, left her coffee in the kitchen, and threw herself into a rigorous routine usually reserved for preparation for competitions or war.

Three hours later, reheated coffee in hand, Sigrid settled behind her desk in her office on the IECS campus, her mind much clearer. Someone had left a stack of DNA test results in her inbox, each one neatly filed in a color-coded manila folder. She selected the top folder, opened it, and began studying the enclosed reports.

As she'd expected, work absorbed every ounce of her attention, and she lost herself in the possibilities arrayed before her. Which Daughters lines were true, which had been altered over time by lost stories or records and the insertion of speculation. Much of that could only be sorted by comparing the records that had survived against the well-documented lineages of other Daughters. Mitochondrial DNA alone could never answer the question as to which Sister a Daughter could claim descent from, or what that Daughter's true heritage was, as the distance in time between ancestor and descendant was too short. Mutations occurred only rarely, on a scale estimated at twice the length of time between the modern era and the time in which the Sisters lived. Only a chance mutation in Abragni's line sorted her descendants from descendants of the other six Sisters, and it, if Sigrid's hypothesis was correct, had originated in the rumored youngest of the Seven herself.

More testing would confirm that, but only if the eldest of the living elders submitted to the tests.

Genealogical records would aid in the construction or reconstruction of those lineages as well. Sigrid etched a note into her calendar to contact Robert Upton the following Monday, and nearly cursed as a memory popped into her head, of Will telling her of his volunteer work with the Blade's husband.

A knock on her door interrupted the remembrance. Sigrid looked up and found George hovering in her doorway, file folder in hand.

"Hey," he said, and cleared his throat. "That blood you found in Director Upton's house. The one you wanted tested?"

Sigrid stood and eased around the side of her desk. "Do we have results?"

"Yeah, uh. Here." He handed her the file and stuffed clenched fists into too loose trousers, then launched into a rapid-fire explanation. "I let somebody else run the tests first. One of the new staff members? Just to see what he could do, only a couple of oddities cropped up, so I ran them again. That's why it took so long to get them back. I'm really sorry about that. I just thought—"

She touched his upper arm briefly, halting the deluge of words. "I trust your judgment, Mr. Howe." And she did, in genetics above all other matters. There, his judgment could not be questioned. "Walk me through these oddities."

"Well, first there's the fact that whoever this blood belongs to is nearly entirely of Near Eastern descent."

"We have several groups of the People living in that area."

He shook his head and his eyes gleamed. "No, not like this. Most of those individuals show clear signs of intermarriage. Different ethnicities?"

"But not this one."

"Nope. It's like her family originated in the area and never left."

Sigrid pursed her lips together. "Why is that significant?"

"Because it's so rare. Don't you see?"

He shook his head again, jabbed his fingers through overlong bangs, and paced away from her, his steps rapid and light. Abruptly, he whirled and stalked back to her, and his expression was so unlike his normally cowed mode, it startled her.

"Ok, look," he continued. "We know the Sisters lived about

ten thousand years ago, right? And that they originated in the Levant, probably somewhere near where agriculture first arose. Or that's what I got from the Legend of Beginnings when I read it."

"It's probably an accurate portrayal," Sigrid murmured, though she'd never thought of it quite like that.

"So when the Sisters were cursed, what's the first thing they did? According to the genetic records and the tales I've heard."

She narrowed her eyes on him. "Have you been digging around in the Archives?"

He shrugged. "Tom has and, you know. He tells us because we're all in this together, right? I mean, what use is it to withhold information when sharing could expedite the whole process, help us reach better conclusions faster?"

She considered him for a moment, weighing his words. Rebecca had informed Sigrid of her intentions prior to reading the IECS's resident male scholars in on the People's largest secrets, but there had been no mention of the men colluding with one another. Still, it was a wise move on all their parts, though she could wish her young assistant had kept her in the loop as well.

Finally, she nodded. "Go on."

"Ok, so the first thing they did was scatter, or one of the first things. Not right away, no, but within a couple hundred years. Genetically, record wise, and I'm talking oral tales here, passed down until they could be recorded."

"Of course." She'd written down several such tales herself after learning to read and write half a lifetime ago, tales of her own life and those passed down from mother to daughter through generations. "You have a point here, I assume."

"Getting there. These Sisters or their Daughters bred with local populations wherever they landed, diffusing the genetic ancestry of their children. The Sisters and the oldest Daughters died off, those that would've been genetically Near Eastern, or as close as we can determine, anyway."

A budding excitement plucked at Sigrid. She tamped it down, refusing to jump ahead of him in the face of scientific reality. "Ethnicity derived from genetic testing is uncertain at best. The results can be, and often are, incorrect depending on the methodologies used."

"Yup," he said, his young voice emphatic. "That's why I waited so long to bring this to you. I had to be sure, right? So I studied published papers, searching for anything that would help me figure out how to be exact, and at the same time, I went through every single DNA sample we have on file that's been tested, and you know what?"

Impatience joined the excitement. She arched a single eyebrow, expecting him to wilt, and marveled when he plowed ahead.

"Of the samples taken from living individuals—" His mouth twisted into a grimace. "Er, you know. Not from swords and such."

"George!" she said. "Get on with it."

"Right. Sorry." He rocked back on his heels and grinned at her, every inch the excited scientist. "Of all those samples, only a few were as close to being Near Eastern as this one. Wanna guess who else?"

She snapped her mouth shut over a sigh. "Mr. Howe, please."

"All right, all ready," he said, but his grin never faltered. "The Oracle, ok? And, bonus points, she carries that odd mutation in her mitochondrial DNA."

The significance of his discovery appeared to her almost immediately. She dropped the folder on her desk and leaned against it, doing her best to stifle the emotions racing within her, and when that didn't work, she stated her conclusion aloud. "They're old."

"Oh, yeah. Like, Sisters old, or really close."

"The Sisters died millennia ago," she corrected, more out of habit than intentional thought. "But these women could be their

70

Daughters, or could have lived at a time when the Sisters were still young."

"Not long after the curse was implemented, unless I'm mistaken, and I don't think I am." His grin faded, and with it, the ramrod stiff posture he'd assumed during his explanation. "Look, maybe I'm jumping the gun here. Maybe I missed something or—"

She cut him off with a slice of her hand. "Trust your instincts, George, and your work. I do."

His eyes shot to hers and his mouth slackened. "You do?"

"Of course. If I didn't, you would never have been allowed to set foot here."

"Right," he said, drawing the word out. "Ok, then. Do you want me to dig a little deeper?"

"Can you?"

"Yeah. Archaeogenetics is kind of a hobby of mine."

She shook her head and nearly laughed. Of course, it was. What other hobby could a prodigy like George have? "We should celebrate."

"Really? Wow. Um, ok." He rubbed his nape with one hand and tucked the other in the pocket of his trousers. "We've never celebrated anything before. Is this that big a deal?"

"Yes, it is. Think of what we could learn, of all the history these two women can share."

If the one could be tracked down and the other persuaded to talk, but that was immaterial to the point at hand, and a problem for Rebecca to solve anyway. Sigrid glanced at her watch, and did laugh then. It was nearly five o'clock, a perfect time for an early meal.

"Supper and a drink," she declared. "On me. Is The Omega fine? I'm supposed to meet Will there later."

George's shoulders hunched and his head drooped. "Oh, uh. No, that's ok. I'll just go on home."

"And miss our celebration?" She clucked her tongue gently. "Come now. It's Saturday night. Several of the younger

Daughters will be there. I can introduce you, if you like."

His pasty complexion paled and, impossibly, his posture sank into a morose slump. "I don't want another Daughter."

"Don't want another..." Sigrid leashed her exasperation and attempted a more gentle tone. This child was not a Son, she reminded herself, and as such, needed to be handled with more finesse than she usually reserved for males of the species. "What do you mean?"

"Andrea," he said, the single word so miserably spoken, even Sigrid could grasp the emotion behind it.

"Andrea?"

"The Daughter I was dating."

Sigrid hmmd. She hadn't realized he was dating someone seriously enough for any sort of attachment to form. "You're no longer dating?"

One shoulder lifted under the loose fabric of his plaid button down. "Her term of duty was up. She was a guard here, you know? And she got a better offer after her contract was up and..."

When he didn't continue, Sigrid filled in the missing words. Andrea moved on, breaking George's heart in the process.

Raw indignation filled Sigrid. The men brought here to supplement the IECS's staff were under the protection of the women heading the departments in which they worked, or if not them, then under Rebecca's protection. They were to be treated with dignity and respect, and while matches were encouraged, love or otherwise, the men were subject to many of the same laws and customs as beloved Sons.

Sigrid had no Son of her own, though she'd had several grandsons over the centuries, enough to understand exactly how hard their lives could be when a Daughter spurned them.

"Look at me," she said, and waited until he obeyed before continuing. "You will come with me to The Omega where we will order a hearty meal and you will relate every detail of your time with this Daughter to me."

He opened his mouth, likely on a refusal, and she shushed him with a tersely spoken, "No arguments." It was time she assumed full responsibility for her assistant, as was her duty, and past time she helped him overcome this heartbreak, one way or another.

BY THE TIME Will arrived at his parents' bar at four that afternoon, the sky was overcast and the air held the distinct bite of snow. Inside, men and women alike huddled near the TV hung in one corner of the main room, watching a fast-paced college basketball game. Both pool tables had games going, and a third of the dining tables held small groups chatting over beer and finger food.

Eric was manning the bar again. Will caught his eye and waved, then met the other man at the end of the bar. "How's school going?"

Eric shrugged broad shoulders under his black company polo. "It's school. Why?"

"You up for extra hours on a regular basis?"

"I told you, man. I can always use the duckies."

"Get me your class schedule for this semester and we'll work something out."

Eric dropped his chin and stared at Will through thick, black eyelashes. The onyx plugs in his earlobes flashed above the black line tattoo inked into his neck. "Is this about all the people coming in? I mean, we always get a couple of new faces every week, but never this many at once."

Will pressed his lips into a firm line, hesitating as he measured Eric's safety against the People's needs. On the one hand, the mundane mortal was in no real danger as long as he kept his nose clean, and Eric was good at minding his own. On the other hand, if something was coming, maybe it would be better to move him out of harm's way until the storm blew over and life returned to normal, if it ever did.

If there were someone to replace the bartender, Will wouldn't hesitate, but there was no one, and with Will's steadily increasing duties, he couldn't fill in himself.

Oh, the life of a small business manager.

Finally, Will shook his head. "Yes and no. I have some other things to take care of for a while, but yeah, we're probably going to have a lot of new arrivals soon. I'd appreciate the help."

Eric snorted and flipped a bar towel over his shoulder. "Hell, man. You're the one doing me the favor. Do you know how much my student loans are?"

Will clapped the other man on the shoulder. "Two words, man. Trade school."

"Yeah, you tell my ma that."

"I've got my own mom to deal with." And boy, was she going to be interested in what was going on between Will and Sigrid. Speaking of. "You know the tall, leggy blonde who comes in here and bickers with Moira?"

Eric paused in the act of returning to his post. "Yeah, sure."

"When she gets here, send somebody to come get me."

A slow smile stretched Eric's mouth against his honey colored skin. "I'd like me a piece of that."

"Don't let her hear you say that."

"Do I look stupid?" Eric shook his head and wandered off to help a customer, and Will slapped through the swinging door leading to the kitchen.

Work absorbed his attention for the next hour and a half, in between the minor emergencies that always cropped up. Casey popped her head into his office and relayed a message from Eric, who'd forgotten to tell Will they were running short on some of the local microbrews. Wayne, the lead line cook, came in fifteen minutes later and reported that a leak had developed in one of the kitchen's coolers.

Nothing Will could do about either one on a Saturday night. He jotted notes into his calendar and tucked it into his bag. Calls could be made from home on Monday morning when he woke up. No need to come into work unless Casey couldn't make it in that day, and she was scheduled to. Will had a feeling if he started giving up his one full day off, it'd be a long time before he'd get a another break.

About an hour after Will settled behind his desk, his cellphone beeped. He thumbed into the text message, read Casey's warning that Sigrid had entered the bar, and checked the time. 5:23. Hunh. They must be unusually busy out front if nobody could come back and get him.

He shuffled paperwork into piles or folders, then trotted through the backrooms into the bar proper. Sure enough, the tables were steadily filling up. People lined the bar, not so many they were jampacked, but enough to have Eric hopping to fill orders.

Casey scuttled through the nearly full tables, empty tray held high. She passed Will on her way into the kitchen and flashed him a saucy grin. "Welcome to the madhouse."

He grunted, patted her shoulder as she bounced by, and slid behind the bar, automatically filling the spot on the opposite side from Eric. Sigrid was sitting at a table placed against the far wall near the doors. George Howe sat beside her, nodding solemnly as she spoke. Their heads were, unusually enough, bent together. Will snagged a clean mug and held it under a tap of DuckRabbit stout. Work, probably, though he couldn't remember the last time he'd seen Sigrid even acknowledge her assistant in public.

Fifteen minutes later, she rose and eased through the crowd, and settled against the bar near Will, waiting patiently for him to finish with another customer. As soon as he was free, she slid her palm across the bar and gifted him with a rare, soft smile.

"Hello, Will," she said, pitching her voice above the rumble of conversations and an old Stevie Ray Vaughan tune blasting from the speakers. "I must renege on my promise to dance with you tonight. Young George is in need of my counsel."

Will braced his palms against the edge of the wooden bar and arched an eyebrow. "Everything ok?"

"It seems he has been abandoned by a Daughter." Her hand curled into a loose fist against the bar. "You and I will dance another time."

Her voice lilted upward on the last word, forming a hesitant question. Will studied the placid expression on her face, not much different than the one she usually wore, and the proud set of her shoulders under a deep red, fitted sweater. Was she really asking, or was the inflection an accident?

"Sure," he said. "Maybe tomorrow."

She shook her head, sending the end of her long, pale blonde braid slithering over her shoulder. "I am committed to a shopping trip on the morrow and expect to be out of town all day."

"Tuesday, then."

"Not Monday?"

"I'm off."

"Ah." Her eyelids fluttered down, hiding her blue, blue eyes. "Perhaps you could join me for supper on Monday night, if your plans allow."

His heart picked up an extra beat. Will considered her for a moment, even as he warned his wayward heart to behave. "You're asking me out?"

She laughed, a breathy rush of air more than sound. "I thought perhaps you would enjoy a homecooked meal."

"You're going to cook for me?"

"If you like."

He nodded slowly. Dinner at Sigrid's house, just the two of them? Anticipation joined the heat stirring in his gut, and his dick, ever ready for an opportunity, stirred to life behind the fly of his khakis. Sweet Mother, would it always be this way with her?

"Sounds good," he said.

She smiled at him, patient as a hunter tracking game, and finally he took the hint, leaned across the bar, and pressed a soft kiss to her ripe mouth. Her fingers slid across the back of his hand, caressing him in gentle strokes, a reward for his compliance, and the heady taste of her soared through him, filling him with the hard need to draw her close, to take more, and give everything he had in return.

Her hand tightened on his for one brief moment, then she slid away, breaking the kiss, and wove gracefully through the crowd toward the table she shared with George.

Will rocked back on his heels, satisfied to his core. A second date. How in Ki's name would he make it until then?

An unfamiliar Daughter slipped into the spot Sigrid had vacated, snaring Will's attention, and he sprang back to work, busying himself as his mind turned over the upcoming date and the varied possibilities it offered.

Eight

Monday morning, Will parked his truck outside the building housing Robert Upton's office and jogged inside through the light snow fluttering to the ground. It wouldn't stick. The weather had been too warm since the new year, more's the pity. He wouldn't mind getting snowed in later at Sigrid's house, even if he wasn't quite ready for sex.

He grinned, entered the building, and pulled his toboggan off. Well, his body was ready for sex. Hell, he was twenty-eight. A man his age was always ready, willing, and raring to go whenever the slightest possibility of sex cropped up.

His heart, on the other hand, wasn't quite there, not after her flip-flop, and especially without some assurance on her part that she wouldn't do it again. Asking a Daughter for constancy was like trying to lasso the wind. Still, he had to try, for his peace of mind if nothing else.

Robert's door was open when Will walked up. The older man was seated behind his desk, head bowed toward a file. Will knocked on the doorframe and said, "Busy?"

Robert looked up and the concentration on his face eased into a welcoming smile. He flipped the file in his hands closed and wiggled it at Will. "A summary of James Terhune's DNA results. He's descended from a Daughter."

Interest stirred in Will. He closed the door behind himself and dropped into a chair in front of Robert's desk. "You don't say."

"I've been doing some preliminary work on his lineage, just for fun, but now it looks like I'll have to get serious about it." Robert dropped the folder onto his desk and leaned back in his chair, still smiling. "Which means I'll either need an extra set of hands on this, or I'll have to hire somebody."

"Normally I'd volunteer, but right now I'm swamped. Your wife has given me a very long to-do list."

A twinkle entered Robert's eyes as he shook his head. "You'd think she'd be content pressing her honey do list on me and leave you young bucks out of it."

"I've never met a woman who could resist the temptation to order men around, no matter who they are," Will said wryly, and Robert chuckled.

They segued into a long chat about the confluence of Sigrid and George's work with Robert's, and Will ended up lending a hand for a good hour, brainstorming records and researchers with Robert, fetching files to save the other man's deteriorating muscles some wear and tear, and learning, always learning. The forgotten paths between parent and child down through the generations had always fascinated him. Who were those people? How had they lived? What were their dreams and thoughts and goals?

Extant records could only go so far. They couldn't answer the questions he most wanted answers to, but they could serve as guideposts for speculation and possibly aid researchers in their quest to reconstruct an individual's life.

So much had been lost.

He shook his head as he filed folders away in their respective drawers. The People weren't the only ones with a shattered history. Thank the Great Lady they now had the resources to piece together their past in some small way.

Later, he grabbed a quick lunch at his apartment, threw on some old workout clothes, and headed to the Rec Department in Tiger, just south of Clayton. He and Ethan snagged a court and indulged in a rough and ready game of basketball, ending just as school kids wandered in for some afterschool time on the court.

They left the kids to it, snagged their gear, and headed out side by side to their cars, parked together under the cloudy February sky. Ethan opened his car's door and crossed his forearms on its roof. "Ready for your date?"

Will stifled a groan as he opened his truck's door and threw his duffle full of gear inside. He should never have encouraged his cousin to come out to The Omega on Saturday night. Ethan had taken a great deal of pleasure from heckling Will about his sudden popularity, especially after Will let it slip that Sigrid had invited him to her house for dinner.

"Don't you have somebody else to bother?" he asked.

"But you're so easy to tease." Ethan slapped a hand against the roof. "Don't do anything I wouldn't do."

"That leaves a lot of wiggle room," Will muttered.

He got in the truck, slammed the door shut. Cranked his truck's engine and let it warm, and waved at Ethan as the other man pulled away. The game had held Will's attention long enough for him to forget about the night ahead. Now that it was over, anticipation roared into him full force, and with it every doubt he'd ever had.

He shook them off as soon as they popped into his head. Wallowing in what ifs was unproductive, especially when his mind drifted into the negative. Much better to consider the positives, like what Sigrid would be wearing and whether she'd let him kiss her again.

No, he *would* kiss her. He had to put his foot down at some point with her, and that was as good a place to start as any. He would kiss her, if the time was right, and when it was, he'd coax her into touching him, leading her where he wanted her to go instead of waiting for her to set the pace.

Daughters usually didn't let a man lead. Too bad. He wasn't going to sit back and let her toy with him any more than she already had. If that meant breaking tradition and going against everybody's expectations, tough. Damned if she'd break his heart the way she had every other one of her lovers.

Will put the truck in gear and eased out of the parking lot toward home, busily planning exactly how he could bring Sigrid around to his way of thinking.

SIGRID ADJUSTED the rose and Asiatic lily centerpiece placed in the center of her dining room table. The mixture of red and pink flowers, touched here and there by purple waxflowers and multi-colored lily of the Incas, warmed the space as much as the two flickering candles set on either side. Soft piano music played on the TV, a random sampling of composers courtesy of Pandora, and a fire crackled in the living room's fireplace. Everything was perfect.

She smoothed a hand over the black dress she wore, soothing her nerves. It was new, this dress. She'd found it yesterday during her planned shopping trip with two of her daughters and their families, one immortal, the other not. When she'd seen it displayed in the boutique's window, her mind had fallen to Will. Would he appreciate the dress's tailored cut, the soft drape of fabric across the tops of her breasts, the easy swish of the flared skirt above her knees? Would he wonder what she wore underneath, and attempt to discover that for himself?

A laugh stuttered out of her, unbidden. When had she ever worried over a man's attention? When had a man ever mattered enough to consume her thoughts, as Will did?

The doorbell rang, knocking Sigrid out of her reverie. She checked the time on the slender watch fastened around her left wrist among silver bangles. Punctual, exactly what she would expect from a Son of his breeding.

She smoothed her dress down one last time, fixed a haughty expression on her face, and marched to the door, her heels tapping with each step across the hardwood floor past the carpet protecting the dining room floor.

She swung the front door open wide, letting in the evening's chill. Will stood on her stoop, protected from the flurrying snow by the wide porch separating the house from the yard. He wore a black wool coat buttoned up over dark brown slacks and held a custom sized wine bag in one hand. Snow melted in his thick blond hair and a smile shone from his light green eyes.

She stepped back, allowing him entrance, and frowned at the flurry of nerves jumping in her stomach. Before she could subdue them, Will slid a hand around her waist, bent his head, and pressed a soft kiss to her mouth. She relaxed against him, accepting his touch and the heat it stirred within her, awash in the pleasurable slide of his lips against hers.

He nipped her lower lip, kissed the slight pleasure-pain away, and drew back, a warm smile curving his mouth. "I brought the wine."

She shoved the door shut, so rattled by the unexpected greeting, it was all she could do to thank him and take the bottle from him while he shrugged off his coat and hung it on the hook by the door.

He pried the bag out of her suddenly numb fingers and placed a hand on the small of her back, guiding her gently into the room beyond. "Something smells good."

Dinner. Yes, of course. That's why he was here, after all, to partake of a meal. "Butternut squash soup, roast chicken, and winter vegetables, and for dessert, a chocolate and raspberry tart."

"Sounds delicious. Where do you want the wine?"

"Here." She took it from him again, steadier now that she'd gotten used to this newly polished Will with his suave style and poised grace. "Would you like a tour before the meal?"

"Please, but could you do me a favor?"

She paused halfway between him and the kitchen, and arched a single eyebrow. "Yes?"

He stuffed his hands into the pockets of his slacks and rocked back on his heels. "Could we dispense with the formality and just enjoy the night?"

"I thought we were."

A wicked grin flashed across his face. "Yeah, but I don't want to spend our time rocketing back and forth between kisses and polite chitchat. Maybe we could find a middle ground."

As long as it included the kisses.

The thought popped into her head out of nowhere and, unaccountably, warmth touched her cheeks. She swiveled away from him, hiding the blush, and set the wine on the kitchen counter. When she was certain the color had faded from her cheeks, she returned to where he stood, still grinning, and looped her arm through his.

"Be at ease, Will, here in my home."

"I'll do that."

He slipped his hand out of his pocket and joined it with hers, twining their fingers together in a loose tangle. His palm was warm against hers, his touch gentle, and his attentiveness unwavering as she introduced him to each room within her home, the kitchen and living areas, the study and the many books she'd gathered over her life, as time and money allowed. The weapons lining the hallway, the guest bedrooms upstairs and down, and her personal space, the one room that was hers and hers alone.

His gaze lingered on the feminine yellow bedspread decorated with splotches of red roses, on the filmy curtains layered over the windows along two walls, on the antique sleigh bed and matching furniture, and his green eyes darkened as they glanced from her bed to her.

Would he lead her there tonight?

His thumb slid over hers, a sensual glide of warmed skin, and desire swirled within her, taking her breath.

"We should probably eat now, yeah?" he murmured, and she took the opening he gave her, somehow both glad for the reprieve and disappointed by the reminder.

Over the meal, they chatted about her work and his, skirted around his childhood, and landed squarely on hers halfway through dessert.

"Amma doesn't talk much about growing up a Viking," he said.

"It was a difficult time." She scooped up a sliver of the tart with her spoon and allowed it to melt on her tongue before continuing. "I'm a few years older than your grandmother."

"I know."

"You do?"

"She told me. Amma did. She told me a lot of things." His gaze was steady on hers, knowing, and just a little discomfiting. " 'For thou seest the fate that to gods and men is given. What sign is fairest for him who fights, and best for the swinging of swords?' "

Her spoon clanked against her plate and her eyes widened. "Reginsmol."

"I took a class on Vikings in college and, of course, we studied some of the eddas and sagas here at Tellowee." His shoulders rolled under his crisply pressed, eggshell colored shirt. "Some of it stuck."

But to remember such an obscure passage from the Ballad of Regin, and from an older translation at that, an outdated translation in which the scholarship had long since been corrected by other, more modern scholars. Sigrid struggled for a moment, torn between remarking on Will's usage and being impressed by the depth of his knowledge.

Before she could decide either way, Will pushed back from the table and held out a hand to her. "Dance with me."

She blinked up at him, caught unawares by the sudden subject change. "Dessert—"

"Later."

The roughly spoken word slithered along her skin, leaving a trail of heat in its wake. She placed her hand in his and rose, and went willingly into his arms. "I've never danced to Satie before."

Will tucked her against his chest and brushed his cheek along hers, suffusing her in heat and the masculine tang of his cologne. "I like his gymnopédies. They're soothing and sensual in a quiet, melancholy sort of way, like you."

She laughed into his throat. "No one has ever accused me of being soothing before, or quiet."

"On the battlefield, no. Probably not at work, either." His shrug cushioned her face briefly between his shoulder and cheek. "But here, you're feminine and beautiful and everything a man could want. I love your dress."

She'd bought it for him. The words clung to her throat, refusing to escape.

"I waited as long as I could, I swear," he said, then his mouth was on hers again and his hand slid up her back and tangled in her hair, and it fell down out of the careful coif she'd tucked it into, and she didn't care, couldn't think or breathe or feel anything beyond him and the heat he gave her.

He tore his mouth away from hers and trailed desperate kisses down her throat. One hand slid into the bodice of her dress and eased the fabric off her shoulder, and his mouth continued there in gentle nibbles and licks, burning her as surely as fire.

She clutched his head to her and trembled under his touch, biting her tongue to keep from begging, pleading, *Sweet Mother, please let him never stop.* His arms tightened around her waist, bending her back, and his fingers tugged her dress down, then her bra, baring her breast to his gaze. He murmured something low and guttural, and licked her nipple, once, twice, and she gasped his name into the air between them, punctuating the sonorous melody surrounding them.

His breath blew across her wet flesh, tightening her nipple under his attention, and the words slipped from her. "Please, Will."

"Always," he said, and the world tumbled 'round as he slid an arm under her knees and lifted her high against his muscled chest. His long strides carried them into her bedroom, away from the music inciting their passion. He laid her gently on the bed, flicked the bedside lamp on, and covered her body with his, easing his way between her thighs.

"I didn't mean for this to happen tonight."

His words took a moment to penetrate the haze of desire ensnaring her in its grasp, and when they did, she froze. "You have no desire for me?"

He huffed out a laugh as his fingers smoothed a stray strand of hair away from her face. "Can't you feel how much I want you?"

She could, there in the juncture of her thighs, where his erection prodded her core through the layers of their clothing. "Yet you have no intention of easing your arousal."

"Not tonight, no. Tonight was supposed to be about getting to know you, figuring out what you want from me and if I'm willing to give it."

His words stung more deeply than they should have. "If you're so unwilling, why are you here?"

"That's not what I meant." His sigh feathered over her skin, the tip of his nose touched hers. "We can dissect it another time, ok? Let me touch you for a while. Please, baby."

His quiet plea, an echo of hers only moments before, melted the hurt, erasing it completely. "Yes, Will. Touch me."

"I'm going to. Merciful Ki, you're so beautiful."

As was he. She opened her mouth to say so, and lost the words to his kiss. It was greedy and hot and rough, and she welcomed it, welcomed him and the desire he coaxed from her, and the heat, Sweet Goddess, the heat overwhelmed her. It rose within her, surrounded her, *was* her, and she marveled at what he'd given to her, and was giving to her still.

His hand slid under the skirt of her dress, paused at the top juncture of her silk stocking and the bare skin of her thigh above it, and his breath hitched audibly. "Are you trying to kill me?"

She laughed and urged his hand higher, laughed again when his next words were garbled against her skin. His fingers slid across her thigh and under the lace thong she'd worn just for him, and found her wet heat so easily, she would never have guessed it was their first time together.

Abruptly he backed off the bed and yanked at his tie, his gaze hot and dark and ferocious in his need. "I'm taking you just like that."

Her hands fell to the bedspread and tightened on it. "Let me touch you. Let me undress you."

He shook his head once. "You touch me and I'll never last."

He jerked the tie over his head, ripped open his shirt, popping buttons off, and tugged at the belt holding his slacks in place. As soon as it was undone, he unfastened his slacks and crawled back onto the bed, still half dressed, settling himself between her thighs.

"Next time," he breathed into her skin, and a moment later, he curled his hand around her thong and yanked hard, breaking the fragile fabric, and then the tip of his erection prodded her core and he eased into her, stretching her with every delicious thrust of his hips against hers as he worked himself into her.

"Sorry, baby," he murmured. "Waited too long."

She wrapped herself around him, cradling him to her. "There's nothing to forgive."

The words were lost to him, she thought, lost in the sensual heat carrying them both along the music drifting into the bedroom.

He thrust once more, grunted as he seated himself fully, then propped up on one forearm beside her and captured her gaze with his. "Ok, I can think now."

She laughed in spite of herself. "We must be doing it wrong, then."

"Oh, we're doing it very right." As if to prove exactly how right they were, he eased his hips back and thrust into her, hard. "I was desperate to be in you, and then that dress and the stockings and the garter belt."

"Too much?" she asked archly.

His mouth curved into the dimpled smile she was beginning

to love. "Just right. Ready, love?"

Yes, she thought, but he was already there, moving his hips in a slow rhythm, echoing the gymnopédie they'd begun their dance with. His gaze never faltered on hers and his hand slid down her arm and captured her hand, and pinned it above her head, holding her in place as the storm built quickly around them, lifting her so high so fast, her breath faltered. She clung to him, arching into each of his thrusts, and tightened her body around him, willing him to go faster, harder, more, always more with him, every moment better than the last.

And it was, so much better, so good. He shifted above her, resettling himself, and let go of her hand only to find her thigh and pin it high against his side.

"Sigrid," he whispered, and his mouth found hers again, unerringly, and all the need he'd roused joined the centuries of loneliness within her, tangling into a desperate knot only he could unwind.

"Will, please," she cried, and he complied, pushing her up and over the edge in three, swift shoves. Her body pulsed around him, begging for his own release, and there, too, he willingly followed, releasing into her in hot waves she rode until he pushed himself into her one last time, giving her everything he had, and more.

WILL'S BREATH panted out of him and his heart raced beneath his undershirt.

Which he still had on, along with his pants and shoes and every other stitch of clothing he'd worn for his dinner with Sigrid.

Except the tie, of course. That he'd had the foresight to remove.

He laughed into her hair and eased to her side, slipping out of her delicious heat into the cooler air of her bedroom. "Should I apologize?"

She curled into him and tucked herself against him, and her

lips twitched into a smile beneath the smudged mess he'd made of her lipstick. "Do you regret what we did?"

"Never." He kissed her once, hard on the mouth, and smoothed her skirt down over the wicked silk stockings she'd worn. "As long as you're ok. Did I hurt you?"

Her smile melted into low, husky laughter. "No, dearest Will."

The endearment shot straight to his heart, piercing it with a hope he'd only rarely dared to indulge in. "Let me get a cloth."

"I'm fine."

He shushed her with another kiss, gentle this time, tender, like a lover should be, in the beginning anyway. Later, maybe they could be rough, but for now, he wanted to show her something different, something better. He wasn't a mundane mortal to lose control the way he had. A Son knew better. Discipline always, even in the bedroom when passion drove a man into primal behavior.

He knew how to treat a woman. The need to prove that to her burned within him as brightly as the desire she stirred so easily.

Why had his heart had to settle on a battle-hardened Daughter?

He shrugged the question off and eased away from her, careful of her lying so calmly beside him. Her bathroom was a reflection of her bedroom, warm yellows and reds, and precisely arranged to suit her exact needs. Will snagged a washcloth out of the tiny linen closet beside the toilet, ran it under hot water, and trudged back into her bedroom, ignoring the loose sag of his own clothing.

She'd turned over on her back while he was gone, and watched him now through the narrowed slits of her eyelids. One hand rested flat on her stomach. The other fell toward him, palm up. She shifted her legs restlessly against the bedspread, and the soft shush of silk on silk brushed along his dick as if she'd stroked it.

Blessed Ki, he had it bad.

He sat beside her on the edge of the bed and nudged her thighs apart, rubbed the warm, wet cloth over her sex, cleaning her, and checked to make sure that no, he really hadn't hurt her.

If he had, she probably would've killed him by now.

The thought should've scared him, or resigned him to his fate, as their first stolen kiss had done. Instead, it only pushed his need for her higher.

He drew away from her, exasperated. Hadn't he already charged in too quickly, fucking her when he'd meant to take his time, draw her out, enjoy the attention she'd granted him?

Her hand caught his in a firm grasp. "What's wrong?"

His mouth thinned. "I shouldn't have pushed."

"When did you push?" The words were mild, uninflected by anger or emotion. "I hoped you would make your passion known."

"It's too soon."

He stood, too restless to sit, and paced into the bathroom. Draped the washcloth over the edge of the bathtub, remembered his own state of undress, and cleaned himself, then yanked his boxer briefs and slacks back into place. When he returned to the bedroom, she was exactly as he'd left her, wanton and beautiful, an ice queen no more, but a woman well loved.

His dick stirred to life behind the fly of his slacks and he cursed under his breath, cursed it and the An forsaken need he'd held for her since the moment she walked into The Omega, every inch the warrior she was.

He'd fallen for her hard, tumbling into a confusing tangle of love and lust and emotion so unfamiliar, he'd struggled to breath under its weight.

And she'd ignored him. For two long, lonely years, he'd watched her come and go, always and forever out of his reach.

Until now.

She stretched her hand out to him, holding it in the air above the bed. "Come to me, Will. Rest beside me for a while."

It was an invitation he couldn't resist.

He flipped on the bedside lamp, a delicate crystal creation, and flipped off the overhead light, then crawled onto the bed and settled down next to her. "We should probably go clean up the kitchen."

"In a while." She turned toward him, as she had earlier, and rested her palm on his cheek. The elegance of her perfume washed over him, something light with the faintest undertone of lilies. "I've never allowed a man to take me as you did."

That surprised the hell out of him. "You don't strike me as a Daughter who lets any man take advantage of you."

"You took nothing I didn't willingly give, but you mistake my meaning. No man has ever overwhelmed me with his strength and passion, with his courage and kindness." Her hand drifted down his throat and chest, and delved under his undershirt, caressing his stomach, arousing him in spite of his good intentions. "Do it again."

The world narrowed to him and her and those three little words. He eased on top of her and buried his face in the soft curls of her hair, and gladly shared his courage and kindness with her until she was sated and satisfied, and in no doubt whatsoever as to the strength of his passion.

Nine

Tuesday morning, Sigrid woke alone in her bed half an hour later than normal. Sunlight streamed through the filmy curtains covering her window, lighting her bedroom, and she stretched beneath the covers, smiling at the aches and twinges of a well-loved body.

The night with Will had surpassed her meager hopes, shaming them. He was a wonderful lover, by turns considerate and playful, rough and tender, and she'd relaxed under his touch, allowing him to coax her into passion as no man had in so long, she'd forgotten.

And her memory was long and detailed and ever bright in her mind.

Only two things marred their time together, his uncertainty, which she had rightly dealt with, and his leaving. He'd snuck out of her bed at a little after two a.m., pleading a busy workload the next day, and she'd offered only a token protest. By that time, her decision had been made. She would approach his grandmother and present an offer for him to her old friend.

What that offer would be, Sigrid was as yet uncertain. That could be settled in the negotiations. Her limits were few where Will was concerned, something she'd discovered when he'd pleased her again and again the night before, often holding his passion in check until bringing her to her own release at least twice.

This was what had spurred Moira to claim her man Tom.

Sigrid's ebullience slipped a fraction, and with it, her smile. She would never submit to Will as Moira had to Tom, no matter how well Will pleased her. Such foolhardiness was beyond her practical nature. Will would become a part of her household, yes, and she would treasure him for as long as his mortality allowed, but she would never cede herself to his tender love. How could she protect him without immortality strengthening her heart and will?

No, she would remain immortal, and if regret mingled with the pleasure lingering in the wake of his touch, so be it. Regret she could deal with. Him coming to harm? Never would she allow that for any man under her protection.

She slipped out of bed and into a hot shower, washed away the remnants of their passion, then wrapped herself in a warm, thick robe and padded into the kitchen. They'd managed to forsake lovemaking long enough to clean up the kitchen, but only just. As soon as the table was cleared and the leftovers put away, Will had trapped her against the kitchen sink, surrounding her with his solid strength, and teased her into an arousal so consuming, she'd lifted her skirt and begged him to take her there, with her hands wet from washing the pots and the dishwasher humming quietly in the background.

Her pussy tightened into muted throbs and her skin tingled from memory alone, a potent testament to his power.

She wanted him so much, had fallen into that need so quickly, it surprised her. But this was Will, sweet, gloriously passionate Will, and regardless of his feelings for another woman, regardless of her past or whatever obstacles were thrown between them, he would be hers.

He'd made his choice last night, and she would never tolerate any regrets on his part, or hers.

She placed a call to Anya's personal secretary and scheduled an appointment with the councilmember for later that afternoon, then ate a quick breakfast and readied for work, certain she'd chosen the best path for herself and Will both.

ANYA BLOODLETTER'S home stood on a quiet residential street along the outskirts of Tellowee. Like many of the historic houses located within the unincorporated town's boundaries, it was large and well-kempt, and had been ruthlessly modernized with every turn of technology's screw.

Sigrid had always loved the two-story Victorian farmhouse Anya had bought not long after meeting her heart's greatest love. She parked her car on the street behind a rental sedan and admired the gingerbread trim decorating the porch eaves, the wide Southern porch, the colorful medley Anya had created in the trim and siding, painted contrasting colors.

It was a lovely home full of love and laughter, even after Anya's husband passed away nearly a decade ago. Sigrid had flown in for the funeral, thinking to comfort one of her oldest friends, only to find Anya not resigned to her fate, but glad for it.

"All those years," she'd murmured to Sigrid during the pre-funeral visitation. "Centuries alone without love. You may think it wasn't enough, the short time he and I had, but it was. You'll see when your time comes, Sigrid. Just wait and you'll understand."

The words had haunted Sigrid in the intervening years, not because of her long and untarnished memory, but in spite of it.

She shook her head, chasing the memory away, and walked regally up the brick sidewalk toward the house. She was halfway there when the front door opened and an all too familiar Daughter exited Anya's house.

Chana Wolfbane.

A foreign emotion squeezed itself around Sigrid's heart. She forced suddenly weak limbs to move exactly as they had before, stopping only when the other Daughter was within speaking distance.

"Chana," she said, and was proud of the firmness of her

voice. "You have business with the councilmember?"

"Of a personal nature." Chana's dark eyes flashed and a secret smile tilted her lips, adding beauty to an already pretty countenance. "I am thinking of settling here in Tellowee."

"Permanently?"

"If all works out as it should."

What force could entice a Daughter to move halfway around the world, outside the seat of her family's control?

The reason hit Sigrid hard. *Will.* She retained control of herself, but only just. Surely she was wrong. Surely Chana's personal business wasn't a potential match with Anya's beloved grandson.

Chana bowed slightly, her gaze never leaving Sigrid's. "I have duties to attend. Well met, kaetyrm."

Sigrid nodded once. "Well met, Chana."

She swiveled around and watched the other Daughter climb into the rental sedan and leave, her mind whirling around the unease growing within her. The front door opened again, a quiet snick, drawing Sigrid's attention, and she turned and continued her journey into the home of Will's grandmother.

Anya was standing in front of a roaring fire in her study when Sigrid let herself into the room, guided there by Anya's assistant. Her steely hair was secured in two long braids, one tucked behind each ear. She wore a carnelian peasant top over worn jeans and moccasins, and stood as erect in her dotage as she had in her youth.

Two steps into the room, Sigrid bowed, much lower than she ever would've to that upstart Chana Wolfbane. Respect had some privileges, after all, and this display was one of them.

Anya turned away from the fire and returned the bow, a smile creasing the skin around her eyes. "Such pretty formality. When was it ever necessary between us?"

"When business deemed it so," Sigrid replied. "How have you been?"

"Old and creaky, but you knew that. Come, sit. Tell me

what's so urgent you had to interrupt my naptime."

Sigrid settled herself on the study's only sofa, a large three-seater upholstered in brown, gold, and green plaids, situated facing the fireplace. As soon as Anya sat down at the other end, Sigrid said, "I have come on a somewhat personal matter."

Anya's cornflower blue eyes sharpened. "It's not like you to beat around the bush."

No, it wasn't. Sigrid inhaled slowly, exhaled on a small laugh. "I'm unsure of my reception."

"We've always been candid, Sigrid, and welcome in each other's company."

"We have," Sigrid murmured, and girded herself for the blunt truth. "I've come to negotiate for your grandson, Will."

Some of the friendliness leached out of Anya's eyes, leaving them cold and a touch haughty. "Have you, now."

"He and I are dating." Sigrid fumbled for the words, struggling to find the ones that would soften his grandmother to her suit. "I believe we would make a good match and wish to bring him under my care."

"I see." Anya studied Sigrid for a moment. Her steady gaze seemed to pierce into Sigrid, seeing right through her to the heart of her intentions. "You understand that this is Will's decision to make."

Some of the tension left Sigrid's muscles. She had expected that, and had the perfect countermeasure.

Before she could speak, Anya continued. "But it is up to his family to ensure that he makes a good decision. Are you aware that another has spoken for him?"

Sigrid only just kept the surprise from showing in her expression. "Chana, daughter of Pari, of the line of Eleni."

Anya nodded. "She makes a good case. Her reputation is spotless, her finances well in order. I believe she would treat Will very well, and possibly even come to love him."

A hard knot of something close to panic lodged itself in Sigrid's chest, stealing her breath. "You have given her permission to court him?"

"As I said, that's up to Will, but I am receptive to her suit." The warmth bled from Anya's expression. "I love you as a sister, Sigrid. On this you should never doubt, but I would rather you leave him be."

"Why?" The word escaped from Sigrid in a breathy rush of confusion. "It would be a good alliance, a further cementing of our long friendship."

"True, but it would also destroy him. I know what you do with your men." When Sigrid tried to protest, Anya waved a single hand, silencing her in mid-word. "Don't deny it to me, old friend. I've been there beside you too many times to give my grandson over to your care. I will not allow you to break his heart."

"I would—" Sigrid swallowed down her words, sure they would only hurt her cause. When she could speak around the rawness gathering in her throat, speak past it and the thought of never having Will again, she said, "Will you stand in my way, should I continue my courtship of him?"

Anya's mouth pressed into a thin line, and in the long moment that followed, defeat rushed into Sigrid, testing the calm she'd struggled so heavily to maintain. This was it, then. If Anya forbade Sigrid from pursuing Will, she would be forced to comply, else a war would spring up between their families. No man was worth that, even one of Will's caliber. Chana would win his heart, and Sigrid would lose him before she'd even had a chance to plumb the depths of his desire.

At last, Anya said, "It's up to Will, but tread carefully here, Sigrid. You know the consequences of treating him poorly."

"Of course. Thank you for your time." Sigrid stood on surprisingly shaky limbs. "Well met, kaetyrm."

Anya's expression softened into a smile. "Well met, old friend."

Sigrid left while her dignity remained intact, measuring her pace out of habit rather than need, and afterwards sat in her car wondering what she could possibly do to hold Will to her without his family's approval.

REBECCA WORKED steadily on clearing the last of the day's paperwork off her desk, one eye on it, the other on her watch. It was early still. More than an hour remained before the official end of her workday, but Robert hadn't been feeling well lately. The need gripping her to check on him, to assure herself of his wellbeing, urged her into a quicker pace.

She was well aware of time dripping steadily away from them. Would that she had another life to live with him. She would gladly forsake the centuries she'd endured before meeting him, if it meant having him all the longer.

Her cellphone rang, interrupting the steady flow she'd entered. She set down her pen, checked the caller, and relaxed into her chair. "Hello, Dani. How are you?"

"Great. Fine." Dani sucked in a breath and let it out in a huff. "Ok, I'm lying. We've got a problem here."

"Oh?"

"Yeah, see. Remember when Drew dragged Bobby and Dave and Hiro to New York and beat the ever loving hell out of that rat bastard Marco?"

Did she ever. Their actions had cost Rebecca a few nights of sleep, worrying over possible retaliations. Regardless of what Marco had done to her youngest daughter, Retribution could not be taken lightly. "What of it?"

"Well, here's the thing. Lukas is here with Stephen." Music squawked in the background, a horn honked, and Dani's voice lowered to a hiss. "Marco cornered Lukas a couple of days ago, had a squad of goons with him. Don't know how he got them to turn on his brother, but they beat Lukas pretty badly. He's lucky to be alive."

Rebecca sat straight up in her chair, already fumbling for her keys and purse. If Lukas died, they lost more than a stable leader at the head of their enemy, or stable enough. They also lost their only key to gaining the Oracle's trust. "Where are you?"

"On our way to Tellowee."

"Get him to the hospital in Clayton. Have Dr. Phillips look after him. I'll be there as soon as I can."

Rebecca hung up and hurried out of her office as fast as her heels could carry her, snagging her overcoat on the way. Her secretary merely waved as Rebecca flew past, and once again, Rebecca thanked her lucky stars the People reared their children to smoothly handle whatever situation was thrown at them.

Half an hour later, she marched into the Emergency Room in the nearby town's only hospital. Dani and Dave were sitting in the waiting room on either side of Lukas Alexiou, who was barely recognizable beneath the bruises swelling his face. His young nephew sat on Dani's lap, holding tight to Rebecca's adopted daughter, his eyes closed.

Dani glanced at Rebecca, then down at the boy sleeping soundly in her lap. When she spoke, her voice was calm and even, hiding any emotion she may have felt. "He's a little out of it right now."

"Nonetheless." Rebecca knelt in front of him and placed a gentle hand on Lukas's jaw. "Can you hear me, Mr. Alexiou?"

His face turned toward her, though his eyes remained swollen shut. "Nala."

"She's safe. We're getting help for you."

"Nala," he repeated, and struggled against the restraining hand Dave placed on his arm. "Stephen."

"We have him. He will receive the best care, I assure you."

Lukas sagged against Dave. Rebecca withdrew her hand and perched on the chair next to Dani. "Why did he come here?"

Dani shrugged. "Nowhere else to go, I guess. He trusts Dave."

And wanted to secure his position with Nala, as he called the Oracle. "Still, I question his arrival now of all times. How certain can we be of his claims?"

"Certain," Dave said in that low, gruff voice of his. "Marco's a dick."

"You should've taken care of that when you had the chance," Rebecca snapped, then hissed in a breath, reining in her frustration.

"Thought we had." Dave's massive shoulders rolled under his thin jacket and he scowled at Rebecca. "Pinico's probably backing him."

The uncle, brother to Lukas and Marco's father. Rebecca rubbed cold fingertips into the headache forming behind her brow. Just what she needed, a rift in the Shadow Enemy. What else could possibly go wrong now?

"Sanctuary," a rough voice croaked.

It took Rebecca a moment to understand that Lukas had uttered it. She glanced at Dani, one eyebrow arched, and Dani shook her head and shrugged.

"Please," Lukas said. "Stephen."

Rebecca sighed. If Lukas had really come here asking for Sanctuary from his family, how could she possibly turn him down, particularly with a young innocent in tow? The People needed Lukas's connection with the Oracle, needed him to help them reach the woman they'd revered through the centuries, if only to learn who she really was. She had so much to teach them, did his Nala, but without him, they would be utterly lost, for Nala refused to speak to any save him.

Ethan strode in just then carrying a duffel and wearing street clothes. He jerked his chin at Rebecca. "Give me ten. I'll go ahead and have him moved to a bed."

"Thank you, dear." Rebecca retrieved her cellphone from her purse and stood. To Dani, she said, "I'll be outside in my car. Come get me if there's any change."

Dani nodded and tucked Stephen closer to her, and Rebecca left, her mind whirling through all the things she needed to do to prepare Tellowee for providing Sanctuary to the leader of their enemy, should such a possibility come to fruition.

100

Ten

The Omega was unusually full by the time Will arrived at four on Tuesday afternoon, half a day after dragging himself away from Sigrid's warm bed. He could've stayed, would've if he were more certain of her. It had been a great night, true, and she'd enjoyed the hell out of it. He'd made sure of that, after his first desperate rush to have her. She'd been well sated by the time he left and loose as a limp noodle.

He grinned as he took over from Eric at the bar, spelling the other man for a well earned break. She was supposed to come in tonight, and when she did, if he could sneak away for a dance with her, he would. That could be his break from work, holding the woman of his dreams close, touching her, bathing in her scent, kissing her.

His blood hummed underneath his skin. Oh, yeah. There'd definitely be kisses.

Will stayed on the floor after Eric returned, greeting new arrivals, directing them to the best places to find shelter and food, and mentally tallying each one against the supplies starting to pour in to the IECS's storage, located deep within the Archives. He'd spent the morning overseeing shipments, unloading trucks, and stacking boxes, and should've been worn out, thanks to a lack of sleep and excess physical exertion.

He passed a freshly built stout off to a customer and tried

hard not to grin. Oddly enough, excitement buzzed in his veins, fueling the work he had to get through before he could crash. Another long day tomorrow. More trucks coming in, more new faces, he'd bet, and another shift at The Omega, maybe capped by a daily dance with his woman.

If that was the routine he'd be following until whatever storm was coming their way passed, he didn't mind one bit.

An hour before the supper crowd usually straggled in, his grandmother strolled into The Omega. Will passed off bartending duties to Eric and walked around the bar into the main portion of the room. Anya met him halfway and turned her face up for a kiss.

Will went one better and added a hug to his peck on her cheek, then eased back, his hands still cupping her shoulders. "What's wrong, Amma?"

A mischievous grin lifted her expression. "Who says something's wrong? Can't I come visit my favorite grandson when I'm of a mind?"

"That would fly if you came in here more often."

He slid an arm around her shoulders and squeezed, mindful of her fragility. She'd always been strong, a force to be reckoned with, and mortality sat well on her, but she was old in a way Sigrid was not, physically old, their great age notwithstanding. The perpetual youth granted by An's curse was gone now, broken by her heart's truest love, allowing Anya to age as mortals did, as he did.

He grimaced. That's just what he needed right now, a reminder of one of the biggest hurdles standing between him and Sigrid.

Anya placed a cool hand over his. "I do need to talk to you, if you have time."

He cut a side-eyed glance at her. "I knew something was wrong."

"Subtlety must be passing me by in my old age."

"Age doesn't have anything to do with it," he said mildly,

and earned a reprimanding pat from her.

He took her to his office through the hustle and bustle of waitstaff and kitchen help preparing for the evening meal, closed the door behind them, and sat down on the sofa beside her. "So what brings a councilmember to my humble bar on a Tuesday evening?"

"I'm not here as a councilmember. I'm here as your grandmother and the head of your family." Anya turned toward him on the couch and curled one leg under the other. "Chana Wolfbane visited me today."

"Oh?"

"She wishes to court you."

Will's eyebrows shot up. "That's the first I've heard of it."

"She struck me as being..." Anya's grin reappeared, wider now. "Old-fashioned. I gathered she expected me to make the decision, though she took it well when I said it was up to you."

It hadn't always been. At one time, a Son, especially a Son as well-connected as Will, would've had his entire life arranged for him from birth to death, often without his having a say in any part of it.

Was he ever glad to've been born in an era when such customs were no longer strictly followed.

"Is there a chance you'll consider her suit?" Anya asked.

The previous night popped into his head. Dancing with Sigrid in her dining room, carrying her to her bed, making love to her again and again and again until they were both spent. Arousal swept through him, so swiftly his breath stalled. He rubbed a fingertip along his temple and forced himself to breathe, just in case his grandmother was still as sharp as she'd always been.

She stretched a hand toward him and brushed it across his knee. "There's another?"

Well, damn. A Son couldn't get away with anything around this bunch.

He considered the situation carefully, turned it around and around in his mind searching for the best response, and finally said, "There could be."

"Sigrid Glyvynsdatter?"

Why was he surprised? They'd been seen dancing together. His truck had been parked outside her house until well past midnight last night. Gossip was bound to reach his grandmother eventually, and through her, his mother.

Anya sighed and tightened her grip on his knee. "You care for her."

How could he deny it? "I do."

"Will, darling." Anya sighed again and withdrew her hand, and her expression was more one of regret than disappointment. "She's asked for you, you know."

Surprise huffed out of him on a short laugh. "What?"

"Sigrid approached me this afternoon and asked permission to court you. I told her the same thing I told Chana, that it was up to you."

"You did?"

"My first instinct was to reject her."

Panic shoved him off the couch onto his feet. "No, you can't."

Anya arched a single, gray eyebrow. "I can't?"

"No, I mean, wait."

He shook his head and paced away from her. Sigrid had actually offered for him? Why hadn't she asked him about it first? He nearly smacked his forehead. Of course, she wouldn't ask him. A Daughter of her age and arrogance would never consider asking a mere, mortal man such a thing, but to approach his grandmother with this, to enter into a formal courtship...

Maybe Sigrid did care for him, just a little.

He whirled around and faced Anya. "I love you."

"Ok," she said, her voice even and just a little curious.

"But I want you to butt out."

"Ah. I knew there was a catch." She shifted on the sofa, placed both feet on the floor, and folded her hands in her lap, ever the calm matriarch. "You have feelings for her."

"Yeah, I do."

"Strong feelings?"

He didn't even have to think it over. "Yes."

Her head tilted to the side and her cornflower blue eyes narrowed on him. "Chana Wolfbane is an excellent match. She would bring a considerable fortune to our family, and would protect you to her dying breath. Her mother would make a powerful ally. Having a refuge in Turkey would strengthen our families ties in that region."

"Forget it, Amma," Will said flatly. "I'm not marrying a woman for political gain."

"But you would for love?"

"If I had the chance."

"I was afraid you'd say that." She stood slowly, as graceful now as he ever remembered her being. "I can't give you my blessings for a match with Sigrid, not at the moment. I know her too well and have no desire to see you hurt."

Will regarded her for a long moment. "Will you stand in our way?"

"Sigrid asked me that very same question." Anya shook her head, sending her long, nearly white braids shifting across the red peasant blouse she wore. "I won't come between you. For now."

Relief sighed out of Will and the tension tightening his shoulders bled away. It was more than he'd hoped for, though in all honesty, he'd never envisioned being faced with this decision, not when Sigrid was the Daughter in question. The fact that she'd thought to formally court him boggled his mind, and left him hanging somewhere between wonder and uncertainty.

Which, come to think on it, was exactly where he'd been since that first kiss.

He stepped up to his grandmother, cupped her shoulders, and touched his forehead to hers. "I do love you, Amma."

"I know, darling." She cupped his face in her hands and stroked her thumbs along his cheeks. "I'll have to tell your mother. She'll probably rush home to see to her little boy's wellbeing."

He laughed at that. "Tell her there's no hurry."

"Tell her yourself. She texted me last night, wondering what you were up to. I told her you were busy on Council business."

Which was true enough. It shouldn't have surprised him that his grandmother knew. "I'll call her in the morning," he promised.

He and Anya went back out into the bar proper, him to his duties making sure customers were well satisfied, her to hers greeting newcomers as the councilwoman she was. Will tucked their conversation and its revelations away for another time, though in the back of his mind, he couldn't help dwelling on Sigrid and the surprise of having her seek a formal relationship with him.

EARLY WEDNESDAY MORNING, Sigrid and George met in one of the workrooms set aside specifically for housing and testing the known remains of the Seven Sisters. Three specially designed boxes rested on the long island positioned in the middle of the room, each containing a different set of the Bones of the Just, procured from three different locations.

Pieces of the first skeleton had been hanging on a wall in the nightclub Bones, and were discovered during a battle between Daniella Nehring and her mother, Lilith Cæstus. The puzzle over how the remains of a Sister had ended up there had never been solved, but safe money was on Lilith having had something to do with it. Her secrets had died with her the day her youngest daughter had skewered her to a dance floor, so they would probably never know the whys.

Sigrid would've loved to have been there the day Lilith was killed. She and Lilith had had a couple of run ins over the centuries. The other Daughter had been vicious and cruel, and had been one of the few who could best Sigrid in a bout, fair or not.

Jerusha Mankiller and her now fiancé Drew Martin had discovered the second set of remains in Turkey during their hunt for Sanctuary, positively identified as the skeleton of Marnan, and had provided information on the whereabouts of a third set, the skeleton of Eleni, which had been retrieved from Boston.

George entered the room carrying a box identical to the three Sigrid was studying and set it on the table beside the others. He sat down on a tall stool next to the workspace crossing one wall, file folder in hand. His shoulders were relaxed under his lab coat and a shy smile graced his boyish expression. "I finally have the admixture analyses on the Bones of the Just. Sorry it took so long."

The ethnicity test results, at last. Sigrid perched on a stool beside him. "No apologies are necessary. We're all busy right now."

"Yeah, well." He glanced at the folder in his hand as if he'd forgotten he held it, then opened it. "Right. The results were exactly what we expected. All three show strong Near Eastern origins, nearly pure, as a matter of fact. And guess what? That fourth box there? It's a near match in ethnicity to the other three."

Sigrid straightened on her stool. "Another Sister?"

George shrugged. "Female, same mitochondrial DNA, same ethnic origins, and a remarkable similarity in bone structure from the cellular level out, so she probably grew up in the same environment. If she wasn't a Sister, she was closely related to them."

"Where did you find that?"

"It's the remains Moira found in the Archives a while back. It didn't hit me until I was running the admixture analyses on the Bones of the Just that these remains were very similar."

Was it true, then? Had a Sister's remains been stored here in Tellowee, sheltered from time and their enemies, right under the very noses of those searching for it? Excitement raced under Sigrid's skin. She crossed her arms over her chest and eyed the boxes.

Four sets of bones, possibly four of the Seven Sisters gathered in one of the People's centers? No wonder Rebecca thought the Prophecy of Light was finally coming to pass.

She shrugged the speculation off and returned her attention to George. "Any mutations in the mitochondrial DNA?"

He shook his head sharply. "Sorry, no. They're all exactly the same, just what we'd expect of four sisters born of the same woman."

"So none of these bones belonged to Abragni, though by process of elimination we know two belong to Marnan and Eleni." Sigrid squelched her disappointment and crossed her arms over her chest. "It's too bad genetics can't help us identify which Sisters the other remains belong to."

"Maybe someday, but hey. We're lucky we could get enough DNA out of the skeletons to run tests, and really, without documentary evidence, we'd have no way to say for certain that these *are* the remains of any of the Sisters."

"True."

"I mean, we know they're old. Sure, they are, and we can sort of guess at their ethnic background through the science and technology available now." George twisted around on the stool and faced the protective boxes, excitement radiating from his eyes and his posture. "But if we didn't have somebody's word, if we didn't know through documents or whatever, how could we pinpoint their identities as much as we have?"

Sigrid relaxed against the edge of the work table, doing her best to suppress her humor. "Good thing we have an Archives full of documentation, yes?"

A faint blush brightened his cheeks and his shoulders slumped. "Sorry. I just get excited about the possibilities."

"Don't apologize, George. Cherish your excitement while you have it." The Lady Ki knew Sigrid had lost hers long ago, and rediscovered it only recently in a towheaded Son with beautiful green eyes and a kiss so potent, it left her reeling two days later.

They had danced last night under the fairy lights strung above the dance floor at The Omega.

Warmth suffused her, from the memory of his touch, from the anticipation filling her. They would dance again tonight, if she had her way, and since Will seemed unable to deny her such simple wishes, she would. Afterward, perhaps he would indulge her again by spending the night in her bed, or she in his. Where her young lover was concerned, she too had a hard time saying no.

George cleared his throat. "So, anyway. About the other day."

Sigrid arched an eyebrow. In the past, such a gesture would've sent him running. Now he merely continued his rambling thoughts aloud, as had become his habit in the past few days.

"I wanted to thank you for letting me unload about Andrea." He grimaced down at the file folder in his hands and tightened his fingers around its edges. "I shouldn't have said anything. I mean, you're my boss and personal stuff shouldn't bleed over into work, but I—"

Sigrid leaned forward and touched his forearm, stopping him in mid-ramble. "I'm not just your boss, George. I'm the Daughter responsible for your wellbeing during your tenure here at the IECS. You are, in effect, part of my family. If I had no care for you, I would fail myself as well as you."

"You Daughters and your duty." George shook his head, his scowl deeper now. "Anyway, I appreciate it. Talking to you helped a lot."

"I wish you would allow me to intercede on your behalf." She curled her hand around his and waited until he looked at her before continuing. "If you were my Son and truly a part of my family, I would go to Andrea's family and seek Retribution on your behalf."

"But I'm not a Son. I'm not anything."

The sadness in his voice rent right through her heart. "You are more than you believe, George, much more, and I won't have you saying otherwise."

"You won't, huh?" A small smile eased the gloom in his expression. "I guess since you said so, I have to believe it, right?"

"Now you understand. A Daughter's word is law."

His smile turned into a grin, then into laughter, and he chuckled so hard, she could do nothing less than join him in his humor.

When he'd finally wound down, he said, "Thanks. Really. It's a lot better working here, now that I know you're still human."

"Pfft," she scoffed, and tilted her nose into the air, affecting a snobbery she knew well how to use to her advantage, when the time was right. "I am no mere human. I am a Daughter of the line of Bagda, a warrior of the ages, and not one to be trifled with. You would do well to remember that."

"Oh, trust me. I will." He handed the folder to her and tilted his head toward the boxes holding court in the center of the room. "Time for these to go into storage?"

"Not yet." She tapped the edge of the file against her skirt and considered the Bones of the Just. "How is the testing coming for the skeletal remains in the on-site museum?"

George winced and hissed in a breath. "Damn it. I knew I was forgetting something."

Sigrid clucked her tongue. "For this, I shall have to punish you. Next time, the beers are on you."

"You're on. Speaking of, are you going to The Omega tonight?"

She turned her gaze to a search for nonexistent lint on her skirt. "Of course, and you?"

"Wouldn't miss it for the world." He cleared his throat, then said in a carefully casual voice, "Will's a pretty good guy, yeah?"

A slow smile found its way into her expression. "Indeed, he is."

"Maybe you should, ah, you know." He shrugged and a hint of pink rose in his cheeks. "Be nice to him. I mean, the way you were with me."

"I am doing my best," she assured him, then turned matters away from the personal onto work, marveling the whole while about the transformation one simple conversation had had in George's demeanor.

Eleven

As Will had suspected, it was a long week. By Friday, he was ready for some rest and relaxation, or at least another night with Sigrid, just him and her and some alone time. Every waking moment had been dedicated to either his duties at The Omega or his duties to the People.

Except when he could sneak away for a dance. That was something he'd made time for every single night, and looked forward to doing again. Holding Sigrid, even on a crowded dance floor, made every day a little brighter.

She'd asked him to spend the night with her.

He shuffled last year's receipts into a folder and stacked them with the other paperwork headed to The Omega's accountant. Telling Sigrid no had been the hardest thing he'd done in months, harder even than watching her across the room back when she had no clue he even existed.

But it had been the right thing to do. Between her job and his, the time just hadn't seemed right for them to make that leap. Tonight, though, he was going to float it by her, real casual, so she wouldn't suspect how much he wanted to make love to her, then hold her as they slept.

He rubbed a palm over the twang in his heart. Maybe it was too soon, but hell with that. He wanted her too much to let the doubts lingering in his mind stand between them.

A soft knock hit the door to his office. He flipped his hand over, checked the time on the watch strapped to his wrist, and grunted. It was past time for him to be out on the floor. He could spare five minutes for the person in the hallway, then he needed to head out and spell whoever was due for a break next.

The knock came again. Will stood and called, "Come in."

Chana opened the door and stood there, poised in the middle of the doorway, looking more like a model for traditional Persian dress than the fierce warrior she was. "Do you have a few moments?"

"Sure. What's up?"

"I wish to speak to you on a matter of some import." She shut the door, glided across the room, and stopped in front of him. Her dark eyes glinted as she glanced up at him through a fringe of nearly black lashes, coy and enticing and lovely. "Your grandmother has granted me permission to court you, should this be your desire."

Will stared down at her, too stumped by the forthright delivery to muster a response.

"My own mother has bid me to seek alliances here in the West." She placed her narrow hands on his chest and leaned into him, suffusing him with the faint touch of an exotic perfume. Laughter tinkled out of her, as graceful as everything else about her. "That sounds so cold, does it not?"

He managed a smile for her. "Just a little."

"I am not a cold woman, Will Corbin."

"Never thought you were." He wrapped his hands gently around her upper arms, mindful of the silk jacket she wore, this one a deep yellow, and of the delicacy of rejecting a Daughter's advances. "Look, I—"

The door swung open, cutting him off, and Sigrid stepped into the room. He jerked away from Chana, but not before the smile Sigrid wore morphed into a hard, expressionless mask.

He held out a hand to her, staving off whatever storm was brewing. "Wait, Sigrid. It's not what it looks like, I swear."

"What does it look like?" She closed the door behind herself, far too softly for his peace of mind. "I came to speak with my lover and find him holding another woman."

"Not holding," he said, at the same time Chana said, "Lover?"

"Yes, lover," Sigrid said.

Chana glanced at Will out of the corners of her beautiful eyes. "Is this true?"

"Yeah, it is," he said.

"You are mated, then."

"Not exactly." He raked his fingers through his hair, hooked his hands on his waist. "I was about to tell you that I'm sort of already spoken for."

"Sort of?" Chana's gaze cut to Sigrid. "Yet your grandmother seemed willing enough to entertain my suit."

Will winced. Nothing he could say to that. Anya had made her preferences clear, and wherever his grandmother led, his mother, strong-willed as she was, would surely follow.

Sigrid's chin shot up a notch. "I have the prior claim."

"And the requisite permission to court him?" Chana asked archly.

Sigrid hesitated half a second. "Anya is an old friend."

"That's no answer."

"She will not stop me." Sigrid's blue eyes shifted toward Will. "Especially given our relationship."

"That of Daughter and sex slave?" Chana's laughter rang out, no longer light and airy, but hard and skeptical. "The rumors of your past have reached even my ears, Sigrid Deathknell. Your maltreatment of men is legendary. Will would fare far better under my care, as his female kin will agree."

Will held his hands up, palms out. "Now, wait a minute. Who I date is nobody else's business, least of all Amma's."

"But whom you marry is, indeed, of great concern." Chana rolled her shoulders and stepped away from Will, facing Sigrid. "My family needs the alliance with the beloved grandson of a councilmember, and a close cousin of the Blade, and I have high hopes of breaking my long immortality with a Son of such beauty and wit."

Sigrid's sword hand twitched so slightly, he only noticed because he was watching her. "I should've killed you for touching him."

"You could try."

Will skirted the desk and placed himself between them, carefully out of reach of both. "Hold on, now. This is still my decision."

"You lost the right to make this decision," Sigrid said in a voice so cold, goosebumps popped up on his skin, "when you came willingly to my bed. I challenge you, Chana Wolfbane, Daughter of Pari Bakhshesh, of the line of Eleni, for your temerity in touching my property."

Chana stared down her finely crafted nose at Sigrid. "When and where?"

"For fuck's sake," Will muttered. "I'm not letting y'all fight over me. This isn't the fucking middle ages."

Sigrid's eyes flashed fire. "Not your call."

"Fine. Kill each other for all I care." He snagged a piece of paper and jotted down a note to set up a challenge, then threw his pen down and glared at both of them. "I'll make the arrangements, but until then, if I hear even one rumor of y'all exchanging cross words, I'll ban you both from The Omega and make sure Rebecca tacks on a suitable punishment. Deal?"

Chana nodded. "It is agreed."

She bowed to him, then walked out, never taking her eyes off Sigrid until the door closed on her.

Will crossed his arms over his chest, leaned back against the desk, and turned his glare on Sigrid. "What the fuck?"

Her lips thinned into a hard, red slash. "You accepted her touch."

"I did no such thing."

"Her hands were on you."

He tamped down on the anger roiling around in his gut. Getting mad at her would not help this situation, no matter how much he wanted to yell at her. "And? Are you going to challenge every woman who dares to get close?"

"Only the ones who wish to—" Her teeth clicked together, cutting off her words. "You will present yourself to me within half an hour of closing tonight."

He shook his head. "Oh, no, princess. We're not going there."

"We are going," she said through clenched teeth, "exactly where I decide we will go. Present yourself, or I shall hunt you down and chain you to my bed."

"Well, I guess that would be a first," he said, and immediately regretted the sarcasm when she paled and flinched away.

"Half an hour, Will."

She pivoted on the ball of one foot and marched away, and he scrambled after her, his anger gone under the weight of regret.

"Sigrid, wait. I didn't mean it."

She paused at the door and half turned toward him, nodded once, and then she slipped away, as quietly as she'd entered.

Will stood in the middle of his office, hands on hips, and stared up at the ceiling. Sweet Mother, he'd royally screwed that one up. He had a funny feeling the screwing was just beginning, too. Rebecca might welcome an exhibition, but she was sure to pitch a hissy fit about Sigrid's challenge, and his grandmother...

He dragged a hand over his face. Fuck. No way was he coming out of this without somebody taking a chunk out of him, especially if Sigrid managed to lose during her fight with Chana.

Friggin' Daughters and their friggin' honor.

On the bright side, Ethan would get a chance to have a go at Levi now, which would at least be more entertaining than watching two women fight over a man.

SIGRID PACED from one end of her living room to the other. Though she'd spent two hours training after leaving The Omega and should be exhausted, sleep eluded her. Every time she closed her eyes, she saw Will standing with Chana, his hands on the other Daughter's arms as if he were pulling her closer.

Clearly they'd been discussing something, else why had Chana been standing just so, with her palms flat on Will's chest and her body soft and willing?

Something ugly and mean shot through Sigrid. That one would receive her dues come the day of the exhibition. Rebecca would insist on non-deadly combat, and as long as the contest was held within Tellowee, Sigrid would abide by the Blade's rules.

Outside of Tellowee was another matter.

Will was her lover, *hers*, but perhaps he had forgotten that. Perhaps the night they'd shared had meant nothing to him beyond a pleasant reprieve from duty and work.

A sharp ache pierced Sigrid, very near her heart. She placed a hand over it and dropped onto her couch, in front of the embers smoldering in the fireplace. Was that all she was to him, a pastime? Did he still long for this nebulous other woman Moira had alluded to?

A hard fist hit the front door. Sigrid gathered her composure, walked to the door in measured steps, and opened it on Will.

His expression was impassive under the fatigue etched into the lines around his mouth and the shadows under his eyes. He stepped inside and closed the door, flipped the lock, and dropped a backpack on the floor next to the wall.

Words lodged themselves in her throat, refusing to be spoken. Had he had a rough night? How could he betray her with another woman? Did he need anything, water, tea, a soft bed, her touch?

Concern, anger, and something too ephemeral to define warred within her, and finally, she inhaled a slow breath and let it out on the demands she had planned to make of him. "You will please me now."

"Hunh."

His gaze slid down her body, taking in the tightly fitted workout clothes she hadn't bothered changing out of and the touch of pink splashed across the toes of her bare feet. Heat lit his spring green eyes, darkening them as he shrugged his coat off and hung it up, and his gaze bore into her, raking desire through her as surely as his touch.

"Take it off," he said gruffly.

Her hands fluttered along the hem of her sleeveless athletic top, but before she could act, he brushed her hands away and stripped the top off her, leaving her naked from the waist up. He hummed under his breath and cupped her breasts, flicked the pads of his thumbs across her nipples. Heat curled into her through the unfamiliar emotion filling her and she shuddered under the slight weight of his hands.

"More?" he said, and she arched into him, unable to resist the husky need in his voice.

Her tights melted away, replaced by the rough graze of his palms along her skin, the warm heat of his mouth, the rasp of his tongue, the sharp bite of his teeth. He suckled her nipples, dragging her swiftly through a passion so strong, she could only gasp and clutch his shoulders and open herself to his every touch.

His hand slid into the juncture of her thighs, then his fingers plucked her clit, rubbed in gentle circles around it, and she bit her tongue, silencing her need to beg, to plead, to do anything if it meant having him inside her.

His mouth grazed her ear, and he whispered, "Say it."

She swallowed past the raw heat clogging her throat. "What?"

"Say you want me."

His finger slid into her and out, then a second joined it, filling her. The pad of his thumb flicked over her clit, and she cried out, "Yes!"

"Say it," he insisted, and the dark, dangerous tone did nothing to stifle the pleasure he was giving her. "Say you want me."

"I do." Her head fell back and her eyes drifted shut, and in that moment, if he had asked her to face an army of a thousand well-trained men with nothing but her sword, she would've done it for him, only for Will. "I want you so much."

His mouth latched onto her throat, sucking the skin over her pulse, and his fingers moved inside her as his thumb stroked her clit, and she lost herself in his touch, lost herself to everything he was doing to her, to the heat of his mouth and the roughness of his touch and the hard strength hidden under his work clothes. Perfect, glorious Will.

"Come for me," he said against her throat, and she did, peaking so hard, she shuddered against him and would've fallen if not for his arm around her back.

The world shifted beneath her and she was lifted high, so high, and tucked against his chest. She closed her eyes, luxuriating in the swiftness of her release, in his compliance, in the tang of his aftershave tickling her nose.

A moment later, he laid her down on the rug in front of the dying fire. "Have I pleased you, lover?"

She smiled and tucked a hand under her head. "You have."

His fingers found the hem of his shirt and tugged. Over his head it went, only to be dropped on the floor at his feet. "You're sated, then."

Unaccountably, his words stirred fresh desire. She shifted her legs against the rug, rubbing them together in a sensual slide of skin on skin. "I would have the pleasure of your touch again."

"As you wish."

He shucked the rest of his clothes, left them in an untidy pile, and she marveled at his beauty, the symmetry of his form, the muscles stretching under golden skin, the dusting of hair on his chest arrowing into a line leading straight to his manhood.

Sig sucked her lower lip into her mouth. For all his

119

impassiveness since his arrival, she would never have believed it possible for him to be aroused, yet there the proof was, jutting away from his body in a hard erection.

He knelt between her thighs, braced himself above her. The tip of his erection prodded her pussy, and she welcomed him gladly, surrounding him with her touch.

He rocked into her, slowly filling her, ever so gently seating himself deep within her. "Does this please you, lover?"

"It does, Will," she murmured, and only then did she realize how much she must have hurt him with her coldness when he'd walked in the door. How could she tell him that? How could she beg his forgiveness for lashing out at him? How could she plead for a return of his warmth when he was giving so much of himself?

How could she have let her jealousy of another woman's touch, a simple and possibly innocent touch, drive him to close off his emotions?

Oh, Will. What have I done to you?

She cupped his face in her hands and forced him to look at her. "You please me, dearest Will."

A faint smile curved his lips. "Not finished yet."

And so she gave in to him, moving with him as he drove them both higher and higher until they fell over the edge together, holding tight to him and the pleasure he so willingly gave her.

WILL SLID OFF of Sigrid and curled up behind her, reluctant to let her go in spite of the fatigue dogging him. Blessed Ki, what a week, and it was only the beginning of the work facing him. That fact should've depressed him. There was still so much to be done, so many people to help, so many more coming in, if rumor held true. Nobody wanted to miss out on the action, whatever that action was. Immortal Daughters were always up for a good challenge, especially if weapons were involved.

He mustered enough energy to nuzzle the side of Sigrid's throat, breathed in her scent. "You should've made me take you to bed before letting me ravish you."

A breathy laugh huffed out of her. "Did I give you the option?"

"Honey, there's always an option."

He skimmed a hand down her long flank, relishing the sheen of sweat covering her soft skin and the hitch in her breathing. To know his touch affected her did wonders for his ego and the futile hope clinging to his heart. Would she ever submit to him, or was sizzling hot sex the best he could hope for?

Not that he was complaining. The sex was great. Awesome, even, but it wasn't the be all, end all of his dreams, not by a long shot.

She half turned toward him, her eyes downcast. In the flickering light thrown across them by the remnants of the fire, her expression was soft, accepting. Womanly. Desire stirred in him, incredible after the amazing release she'd given him, and the two he'd given her. Would it always be this way between them? Would he always be this desperate for her?

"Stay the night."

Her voice was low, gentle, and underscored by a note Will had never heard before. A plea? An apology? He turned her face toward his and kissed it away, savoring the heady heat rising within him.

She wrapped her hand around his wrist and eased away from him, her blue eyes shadowed. "Will you?"

"Stay with you? Yeah, planned on it."

Her eyes swept up to his, and what he saw there wasn't the look of the haughty ice queen everyone thought her to be, but that of a woman unsure of her way. "Did you?"

"It's Friday. You don't have to work tomorrow. I do, but not early." He brushed a stray strand of hair away from her face, kissed the tip of her nose. "I brought my own soap in case all you have is the girly stuff."

Her lips twitched into what might've been a smile. She slid her leg over his, opening her core to him, and scratched her fingernails lightly over his chest. "Would you consider moving in with me?"

He propped up on an elbow and gazed down at her, perplexed by the very un-Daughter-like request. "What's wrong?"

"Nothing. Why?"

"You're asking instead of telling."

"Should I not?"

"This from the woman who threatened to chain me to her bed if I was late tonight?" He tucked her hips closer against his growing erection, enjoying the frisson of pleasure where the tip of his cock poked against her lower stomach. "Maybe I would've liked it."

"Being chained?"

"Yeah."

An image flashed through his mind, of himself lying spread eagle on top of her bed, his wrists and ankles tied down, and damned if heat didn't throb through him. He slid a hand between their bodies, found her core, and slid a testing finger into her pussy. Hot, wet, tight. Desire swept through him, and with it the ever present heat of longing. Was it too soon to take her again?

Her hand grasped his wrist, stilling him. "You didn't answer my question."

He ran their conversation through his head and tried to pinpoint exactly which question she was referring to, honestly he did, but it was late, he was tired, and his woman was naked and beautiful and so close, he could feel the heat radiating off her skin. "Which question was that?"

"Will you move in with me?"

Oh, right. *That* question. "Let's see how spending the weekend together goes."

She was silent for long moments while embers popped in the fireplace and his fingers eased in and out of her pussy, in spite of her restraining hand. At last, she released him and rested her head on her curled up arm. Her eyelashes swept down, hiding her beautiful eyes from him again, and her fingertips traced random circles on his skin.

"Are you reluctant because of the woman you want?" she asked.

That caught his attention, snapping right through the fatigue and desire roiling in equal measures within him. "What woman?"

"The one Moira said..." She rolled her shoulder in a half-shrug. "She said you'd been eyeing another woman."

Anger caught him unaware, flaring bright. He slid his fingers out of her and caught her chin, forcing it up until her gaze met his. "Is that what you think of me, that I'd fuck one woman while I'm interested in another?"

She shook her head, pursed her lips together, but something lingered in her gaze, something miserable and unbelieving and completely unlike the arrogant Daughter he'd come to know.

He tightened his grip on her chin. "Tell me exactly what she said."

"That you weren't taken, but your eyes, quote, drift often enough to a certain woman."

He let her chin go as the anger faded under humor. "That's true enough."

Sig sucked in a breath and her gaze flew to his. "Then what are you doing here with me, Will?"

"Making love to the woman I've been eyeing since the day she walked into my bar." He rolled her onto her back and settled between her thighs, and brushed his lips against her ear. "It was always you, honey, always."

Her hands clutched his ribs and a soft sigh issued from her throat. "Oh."

"Don't ever doubt me again," he said, then eased his cock into her pussy and gladly demonstrated exactly how much he'd always longed to be with her.

Twelve

Sigrid flipped her braid over her shoulder and studied the inventory sheet affixed to the clipboard she held. Upon waking that morning, Will had made love to her with a passion no less intense for its brevity, and she'd clung to him, unable to resist the lure of his warmth. It surrounded her, thawing the heart she'd thought long frozen, easing the loneliness she hadn't even been aware existed within herself.

Boredom, yes, but Will had an answer for that as well. After they'd shared a shower, while they were dressing, he'd casually mentioned his plans for the day. She'd known before the first word drifted past the sensual curve of his lips that the only way to spend time with him was to, as he put it, tag along with him. Pretending she wanted nothing less than every second he could spare had been beyond her.

Perhaps he'd seduced her too well.

She risked a glance at him out of the corners of her eyes. He was standing not ten feet away, quietly discussing spare rooms for storage within the Archives with one of its attendants. His arms were crossed over his chest, his feet were widely planted on the concrete floor, and his expression appeared rapt. Yet every time Sigrid moved, he shifted toward her, as if guided by an unconscious instinct to keep her close.

She focused her attention on the boxes of canned goods

stacked on shelves along the wall in front of her. That he chose to cleave to her in the face of his grandmother's ambivalence spoke volumes about his dedication to Sigrid, but would his wanting her be enough in the long run?

It was always you, honey, always.

His words skimmed through her mind, leaving shimmers of desire and an unfamiliar emotion in their wake. Moira had mislead her there. By Will's own admission, Sigrid was the woman he yearned for, the Daughter he wished most to claim him, not Chana or another unnamed someone.

Perhaps if Sigrid had paid better attention to him in the first place, Moira would never have felt the need to withhold the truth. Perhaps by now, his family would've accepted Sigrid's place in his life instead of encouraging another's bid for his affections.

Something twisted in her chest, fluttering her heart. She rubbed one hand over the odd feeling. If Chana won their competition, she would also win Will, whether he wished to mate with the other woman or not. In the days of her youth, Sigrid would've killed the other Daughter without blinking an eye. The People were no strangers to bloodshed. It was often the simplest method of solving such disputes, though not always the wisest.

Now more than ever, however, the People needed every sword. There would be no more killing among themselves, not until the shadow hanging over them dissipated.

The attendant left, her boots a bare shush along the floor, and Will settled beside Sigrid, so close his arm brushed hers. "How's it going?"

"Well, thank you." She straightened her shoulders and tapped her ink pen against the inventory sheet. "I'm almost finished assessing the canned goods."

"Assessing, huh?" He tapped a fist to his mouth and cleared his throat, not quite hiding a smile. "I meant to ask what you're doing Monday."

"What would you like for me to do?"

A laugh wheezed out of him. "Do you really have to ask?"

She busied herself with the inventory sheet, eyebrows arched, mouth pursed into a moue holding a hint of teasing humor. "Perhaps I've tired of sex."

"Uh-huh." He swung her into his arms, crushing the clipboard between them, and nuzzled his face into her throat. "I guess I'm just gonna have to work harder, then."

If he worked much harder at pleasing her, she'd melt into a puddle at his feet. Humor blossomed and spilled over into a light laugh, and she accepted his touch, relaxing into his play.

When had she ever had so much fun with a man?

His phone rang, interrupting the heat spiraling through her, and Will cursed under his breath. "Some days, a man just wants to kiss his woman."

A tiny thrill shot through Sigrid. Was that really how he thought of her, as his?

She shook her head and eased away from him as he whipped out his phone and answered it with a roughly growled hello. Inventory. Right. She glanced between the inventory sheet and the canned goods, half her mind on his quiet conversation, the other on the work at hand. Tomato sauce, check. Bone broth, check. She frowned down at the sheet, counted boxes again. Did they really need fifteen cases of tinned anchovies?

"Mom, really," Will said, catching Sigrid's attention. "Don't interrupt your trip. Everything's fine here."

A woman's firm voice echoed out of the phone, clearly audible despite its distance. "That's not what your grandmother said. Two women, Will?"

"No, Mom." He glanced at Sigrid, then turned his back and lowered his voice. "I'm only dating Sigrid."

"Sigrid Deathknell!" Wilhelmina squawked.

Will rushed past his mother's outrage. "I'm not deliberately playing one off the other."

"I should hope not."

Sigrid sighed. Even she could discern the chill permeating

the younger Daughter's voice.

"Your father and I will arrive within the week."

"Mom." Will's breath left him in a rush and he rubbed a hand along his nape. "Ok, fine. Just don't rush on my account."

Sigrid tapped the end of the ink pen once against the clipboard, marking her place. First Anya's disapproval and now Wilhelmina's. The two most important women in Will's life, save his sisters, and that's what Sigrid faced.

She should leave him now, before the situation worsened.

Her heart throbbed and stuttered, and she immediately shook the thought away. She'd never run from a battle before and had no intention of starting now. Disapproval could be overcome, with enough time and patience, and his family won to her suit. Chana would be defeated in their upcoming match, effectively ending the other Daughter's claim, and Will would be Sigrid's until the day he died.

She ignored the tiny spark of regret flaring to life within her. Near immortality and a hardened heart were a Daughter's lot. She'd resigned herself to it long ago, and refused to squander another second contemplating a situation she could never change, even if she wanted to.

THE OMEGA was packed that night, more so than usual, even for a Saturday night in the middle of winter when foul weather drove everyone indoors.

Sigrid leaned against the bar in her usual spot and sipped the lager Will had pulled for her. A college basketball game played on the overhead television. Not her teams, but it was better than watching the crowd.

The skin along her nape tingled. Chana was back there with her kin, likely with her eyes on Will. She could watch all she wanted as long as she stayed put. Admiring a man from afar was one thing, poaching on a claimed man something else.

Sigrid rolled her shoulders, shrugging off the half-truth. Will hadn't been claimed yet, and couldn't be until the challenge she'd issued was met and satisfied. Not here at the bar, no. Here, she would respect Will's wishes and keep the confrontations to a minimum.

Which hadn't been hard to do since Moira had started shunning her.

Sigrid sighed into her lager, sipped it, set the mug on the bar. Losing Moira's support had hurt the worst. She'd tried not to think about it, tried to let it go. Moira's temper was too fickle for any other course of action, but by the Great Lady, having her oppose Sigrid's relationship with Will stung.

What was so wrong with sowing your oats when you were young and heady with your own power? If such youthful indiscretions couldn't be forgiven, no Daughter would ever mate. Never mind that Sigrid had only given up chaining men to her bed a mere fifty years ago. What happened in the past should stay there, at least where a woman's sex life was concerned.

A Daughter elbowed into the scant space beside her and a familiar Irish lilt drifted through the air. "Oy there, Will. Fetch me a water and Tom a DuckRabbit Stout, there's a dear."

Sigrid fixed her eyes on the game. If Moira wanted to ignore her, fine. Two could play that game.

"Heard about yer challenge." Moira turned sideways at the bar, facing Sigrid. "Rumor has it you're doing the nasty with me cousin."

Sigrid deigned to stare down her nose at the shorter Daughter. "And?"

Moira snagged the bottle of water Will set in front of her and sipped it, her vivid blue eyes shrewd. "Rumor also has it Anya Bloodletter turned down yer offer of courtship in favor of the outlander."

Not that again. "Do you have nothing better to do than listen to gossip?"

"Not when it concerns me dearest friends and family."

"You're friends with Chana, then?"

Moira grunted and waggled her water bottle at Sigrid. "Touchy, are ye?"

"Not at all," Sigrid said, and hated the stiffness in her voice.

"Touchy," Moira said firmly. "She's been asking 'round about ye, ye and yer kin and me cousin there. Heard she's training, too, and asked Anya's help in the doing."

Ice coated Sigrid's gut. Anya was helping Chana train for their match? Anya who'd trained with Sigrid, fought beside her the longest, and knew her fighting style best?

Sweet Mother. Chana might actually win.

The knowledge seeped into Sigrid, chilling her to the bone. She glanced at Will, sweet Will with his dimpled smile and a passion so deep, she'd barely begun to explore it. Her lover, her friend.

She cupped her hands around her lager and turned the idea over. Yes, they were becoming friends, that and so much more, but if Anya was truly helping Chana and the other Daughter won, that friendship was lost along with all the tenderness Will had bestowed upon Sigrid.

Moira thumped Sigrid's back, knocking her into the bar. "There now, girly. Ye've gone twelve shades of pasty."

Sigrid hunched over her lager, suddenly weary of it all. Why couldn't she and Will have met in another time and place, when she could simply have carted him off and secured his heart in the traditional manner?

"Never worry," Moira continued. "I've a plan for ye."

Sigrid shot her a disbelieving look, her eyebrows arched high. "You're talking to me again?"

"Pay attention, lass. I've been talking to ye for nigh on five minutes now." Moira hunkered down beside Sigrid and lowered her voice. "Now, here's what ye're going to do."

"Wait." Sigrid glanced at Will hustling from one end of the bar to the other and waited until he was out of earshot before continuing. "What are you really doing here?"

"Helping me friend." Moira's voice was just shy of patient

and had taken on the tone of a mother to a small child. "Think ye need all the help ye can get, Sig."

That was true enough, but it wasn't much of an answer. "Moira."

"Sigrid. What's good for the goose." Moira waggled her nearly red eyebrows and grinned. "Chana's not the only Daughter good at digging up dirt."

Curiosity stirred. Damn it, Moira always sidled around an issue by deflection, but not this time. This time, Sigrid needed to know what Moira's motivations were, in case they came back to bite Sigrid on the arse. "What are you up to?"

Moira sighed. "Ye're going to keep needling me 'til I spill me guts, aren't ye?"

"Yes, I absolutely am. Now spill."

Moira glanced at Will, then leaned closer and whispered, "I've seen the way ye look at him, Sig, and I saw the fear in yer eyes when I mentioned Anya's helping Chana. Ye're in love with him, ain't ye?"

Sigrid glanced away from Moira's probing gaze. "I'm an immortal Daughter—"

"Cut the shite, girly. If ye don't love him now, ye're well on yer way."

That Sigrid could never deny. She nodded solemnly, sipped her lager, and ignored the tightness along her nape. Chana could look. It wouldn't do her any good.

"Dish some dirt for me," Sigrid said. "I could use some good news."

Moira shot her a knowing look, but dish she did, in great detail and length as Sigrid filed every scrap of information away for use in her own training.

TWO DAYS LATER, Will woke up alone in his own bed. He flopped over onto his back and threw an arm over his eyes, blocking out the bright mid-morning light streaming through the curtains and blinds.

He'd spent the weekend with Sigrid, just as he'd promised to do. Their trial run together had gone way better than he'd hoped, in spite of the rocky start on Friday night. But a trial run was all it had been, a simple way for them to see how well they fit together in the day to day.

Waking up beside her had been the next best thing to Heaven. Curled around her body, soft with sleep, her gentle acceptance of his touch, the hitch in her breathing when he slipped into her and pleasured her until they were both sated.

His dick hardened under his boxers. Will grimaced and slung the covers off. No time for that. Today was his day off, sure, but he had things to do, phone calls to make, and a Daughter to seduce later that evening.

He checked his messages, smiled at Sigrid's good morning text, and answered her back in kind. No sooner had he hit the send button than another text beeped through, this one from his grandmother. He rubbed a hand over his head, ruffling his hair, and thumbed into it.

Robert Upton in hospital. Family eyes only.

Will sat straight up in the bed, wide awake, and read the rest of the text. Late last night, Robert had had a heart attack and had been taken straight down to Northeast Georgia Medical Center in Gainesville, bypassing the local hospital all together. He was stable, but weak, and would stay in the hospital until the medicines he was taking for his Multiple Sclerosis could be re-evaluated.

The text ended with a list of visiting hours. Will closed the text and dropped his phone on the bed. Family eyes only. Rebecca must be worried about something if she'd insisted on that, or maybe his grandmother had imposed the restriction for some political reason.

He rolled his shoulders, shrugging it off, and launched himself off the bed. The day-late Valentine's Day dinner he'd planned on cooking Sigrid would have to wait. She'd understand.

Family came first.

Only, the thing was, she was beginning to feel an awful lot like family.

He gathered clean clothes together and stepped into the bathroom for a shower, mentally rearranging his schedule as one part of his mind concocted a plan for all the ways he could make up their missed dinner to Sigrid.

Thirteen

Will arrived at the hospital in Gainesville early that afternoon, after a quick lunch with Sigrid where he'd done his best to explain what was going on without giving too many family secrets away. A crowd had gathered in the waiting area nearest Robert's room, comprised of close family, Rebecca's children and their families, those that could make it in, Anya, and a few other near kin.

Will waded through the crowd, fielding hellos and handshakes, and went straight to his grandmother where she sat at the end of a couch next to Charlotte, Rebecca's next youngest natural daughter. "Hey, Amma. Any news?"

"Nothing since the family text blast." She grasped his hands in hers and smiled faintly. "He's been asking for you. Said you were to go right in, and I quote, no matter what those damn doctors said."

Charlotte leaned her head against Anya's shoulder. "Crotchety is a good sign."

"Better than the alternative," Moira said from a nearby chair, and earned a sharp elbow to the arm from Dani.

Will nodded at the corridor leading to Robert's room. "Rebecca's with him?"

"She needs a break. We've all had a turn, but you know how she is." Anya patted his hands with her wrinkled ones and

133

her cornflower blue eyes twinkled. "Be a good boy and spell her for a while before this crowd gets out of hand and we all stampede his room."

Will bent down and kissed her, whispered a pointed reminder that he wasn't a boy anymore, and scooted through the crowd toward his mentor's room.

He opened the door on a whispered conversation between Rebecca and her eldest, Margaret. They broke off in mid-word and glanced up at him, spearing him with identical, blue gazes, Rebecca's weary, her daughter's coolly assessing.

Margaret stood abruptly, stretching to her full height just a few inches shy of Will's. "That's my cue."

She cupped a hand over Will's shoulder as she passed, and slipped out of the room, her boots silent against the tiled floor.

Will took the hard plastic chair she'd vacated and slid his hand into Rebecca's. "How is he?"

Her hands tightened on his and her gaze strayed to her husband. "Not as well as he should be."

"What can I do?"

"Your duty." Rebecca smiled, easing the sting of her words. "It's all any of us can do until his body decides to heal, or his doctors force it to."

Robert stirred, rustling the sheets covering him, and his eyes blinked open in the room's dim lighting. "You make it sound like I'm on death's door."

"You're entirely too close for comfort," she murmured.

"Bah," he said. "It was just a piddling heart attack."

"And an upcoming surgery." Rebecca sighed and released Will's hands. "I have an errand to run while I'm here, a patient I need to look in on. Stay with him, would you, dear?"

Will nodded and accepted the kiss she pressed to his cheek, and worried over the coolness of her skin. As soon as she'd left the room, he turned to Robert. "What's this I hear about you cursing your doctors?"

Robert's mouth twisted into a grimace against the salt and

pepper of his beard. "Damn doctors. Do you know, they've told me I can only have two visitors at a time? Said any more and the excitement might kill me, like I've been living a quiet life all these years since meeting Rebecca."

"Living with a Daughter provides enough excitement for a lifetime," Will said, tongue in cheek.

Robert barked out a laugh. "There you have it."

"What's the surgery for?"

"Bypass. Nothing to worry over, though I'll probably be out of work for weeks yet." A huge breath sighed out of Robert. He fumbled along the side of his bed, punched the controls, and raised the head of the bed to a higher angle. "I know you're overloaded right now between running The Omega and helping Rebecca deal with everyone flooding into Tellowee, but I need a favor."

Will leaned back in his chair and crossed one ankle over a jean clad knee. "Shoot."

"Can you follow up on some research I've been tracking? It's fairly important or I wouldn't ask."

Will pressed his lips together, considering. "I don't know, Robert. My time is short right now."

Robert grinned. "That's right. I heard you were dating someone."

And there went the rumor mill. Hard to keep a juicy tidbit down in a small town in the dead of winter, when everybody had too much time on their hands.

"Sigrid Glyvynsdatter," Will admitted. "We haven't been dating long."

"Long enough. I can tell by that gleam in your eye."

Since that gleam had been earned the old-fashioned way, with a few sensual rolls in the proverbial hay, Will could hardly deny it's existence. "To be honest, if business picks up any more at The Omega, we're going to be shorthanded."

Robert's shoulders slumped against the sheet cushioning him. "So you don't have time for the research."

"I didn't say that." Will sat forward, forearms on thighs, and rubbed his hands through his hair, mulling over his duties. "Look, I probably should've hired somebody already, and this stuff for Rebecca is not a one-man job. Why don't I look into finding help over the next couple of days? If I can, that'll free up time for the research."

"Fair enough." Robert grunted and shifted against the mattress. "Maybe you could hire somebody to bring me some decent food while you're at it. Rebecca's insisting I eat healthy for a change, and healthy in a hospital is anything but."

Will grinned. "That I can handle. So what research is it that's so important?"

"James Terhune's, among others. I'm trying to fill in some of the gaps in his ancestry, in the hopes of finding more relics like the one Dave's mother gave to Dani."

An armband etched with the Eye of Marnan. Will had heard about the former FBI agent's connection to the People and marveled at the coincidences of fate needed to see such a precious item returned to its rightful place.

He and Robert settled in for a good chat about Robert's hopes for the research and the research itself until a nurse came in and shooed Will out. On his way home, he pulled out his phone and dictated notes on ideas for handling the many responsibilities crowding his plate, on the slim hope of finding a way to fulfill all of them and still have time to spend with Sigrid.

ONCE OUTSIDE Robert's room, Rebecca veered away from the waiting room and the family holding vigil there. Will would send someone else in to watch over Robert when he left, just until she could catch her breath.

An image shot into her mind, of her husband collapsed on the floor, sweat dotting his skin, his body taut with pain, and she shuddered and hugged her arms around herself and uttered a prayer to the Lady Ki.

Please spare him, Great Mother.

If only life were simple enough to be solved by a desperate plea, however reverent.

Rebecca wandered through the hospital until she found a set of stairs, then took them to the floor housing the one man she'd rather never see again. After Lukas had fled New York and landed bruised and battered on Dani and David's doorstep, Dr. Phillips had judged his injuries too great for the local hospital to treat.

Secretly, Rebecca wondered if Ethan had simply wanted to place some distance between his newest patient and the many Daughters angling for his death, a wise move considering Lukas's importance.

She found his room, marked by an innocuous pseudonym to defray the curiosity of passersby, and tapped softly on the closed door. A cultured male voice called, "Enter," and Rebecca did so, twisting the doorknob and pushing the cold door open, though she would rather have been anywhere else.

Duty bade her see to this man's care, even in the face of the Woman's vision of the Blade crumbling under the Shadow.

Lukas was sitting up in his bed wearing a hospital issued gown. A thick, leather bound book lay open on his lap and the room was as bright as the corridor. "Good afternoon, Director."

"Mr. Alexiou." Rebecca shut the door firmly and sank gracefully into a chair at his bedside. "How are you?"

"Better. Dr. Phillips has assured me of my release as soon as appropriate housing can be found." He marked his place in the book, closed it, and rested a piercing gaze on Rebecca. "Have you considered my request for Sanctuary?"

"I haven't made a decision yet."

"Time grows thin, Director. My uncle will not hesitate to attack, as I have, and with Marco egging him on?" Lukas clasped his hands together and rested them on the book. "I'm surprised they're not here already, knocking at the IECS's gates. It's been nearly a week, after all. They've had plenty of time to marshal their forces."

Rebecca arched one eyebrow. "Is that a threat?"

"Merely a reminder of the dire situation we each face."

An unnecessary one. She was well aware of Pinico Alexiou's warmongering, and had been since before Dani had found a stash of weapons linked to Lukas's uncle in a warehouse not far from where Rebecca now sat. "The People have always faced their enemies head on."

"If that is so, why do you hesitate now? I can help you, Director, in ways you cannot possibly comprehend."

Rebecca leaned forward, her own gaze as cold as his. "Enlighten me, Mr. Alexiou. How exactly is it that a lifelong enemy of the People can render aid?"

"Nala," he said flatly. "Allow me to see her. You have much to learn from her, but she will not speak to another."

"Because you've cautioned her not to."

"Because she's a stubborn, arrogant woman and refuses to assimilate to the modern world." Lukas closed his eyes and leaned his head back against the pillow cushioning it. "Much like other elders among the People, yes?"

That was a bit of an understatement. The more a Daughter aged, the less likely she was to adapt to the changing times. The inability to assimilate had led to the deaths of more than one among the People.

"I need to see her." The words were a harsh whisper among the hum of fluorescent lights and the drip of the IV attached to Lukas's arm. "Please, Director. I can help you only if you will allow me to."

Rebecca sucked in a long breath, released it slowly. So much rested on this decision. If she trusted Lukas, the man destined to kill her, and he betrayed the People, how could she ever forgive herself for willingly placing him in their midst? But if she turned him away and Nala continued her recalcitrance, refusing to speak to another, what advantage were they losing?

Never before had she been faced with such a hard choice.

Never before had she taken so long to decide.

"I need time to seek counsel from our ruling body," she hedged.

Lukas's deep blue eyes flew open. "No, you don't. You're stalling, and we do not have time for such tactics."

She leaned forward in her chair, her words hard and merciless. "You're the only one whose time has run out, Mr. Alexiou."

"If only that were so. You leave me no choice, Director, none." He set the book aside, slid out from under the covers, and braced himself against the IV stand, his shoulders thrown back under the stony weight of his gaze. "I challenge you for the right of Sanctuary, and for the right to freely communicate with the woman you call the Oracle."

Rebecca slammed her mouth shut and gritted her teeth together. "Only those of the People have the right of challenge."

"I wear the mark of Nala," he said, each word a deliberate force in its own right, "and am therefore of the People through my union with her."

Rebecca stood slowly and weighed his challenge against the hue and cry sure to follow such a match. Many among the People would be unhappy no matter how it played out, and unhappier still should Rebecca decide to grant their enemy Sanctuary upon defeating him on the mat.

And defeat him she would. Lukas was taller and stronger, his reach and step were longer, but no man was a match for her in combat, and hadn't been since she her days as an untried youth. The People trained hard, fought harder. They had to if they wanted to survive, and she had more reasons to live than most.

Still, it would prove a point. Entrance here must be earned.

Solemnly, Rebecca nodded. "I accept your challenge. We have an exhibition scheduled soon. I expect you to abide by our rules and the challenge's outcome."

He bowed to her, never removing his gaze from hers. "Of

course. Well met, Rebecca of the Blade."

A chill shivered down her spine. Only two people had ever rendered her name like that. One was her adopted daughter Dani, during a vision spoken not long ago. The other was the Woman with No Face, an assassin who was, as far as Rebecca could tell, a Daughter of unknown origins.

Rebecca clamped down on her emotions and returned Lukas's bow, then left before fatigue caused a slip she could ill afford.

MONDAY AFTER LUNCH, Sigrid hunkered down with George and the results of the tests he'd directed their team to run on the skeletal remains housed at the IECS museum. He'd started with the oldest, a sensible precaution given the impetus behind their search. It had been less than a week, but already results were rolling in. She and he had met in the workroom holding the Sisters' remains and worked side by side sorting through and collating data.

The weekend had been pleasant.

Sigrid ducked her head and shuffled paper in a half-hearted attempt to hide her happiness. Will had spent much of his time at work, either coordinating supplies and the housing of visitors, or at The Omega. At night, though, he slipped gladly into her bed and shared it and his pleasure with her, even when fatigue sent him straight into sleep afterwards.

He was doing too much.

She was reluctant to discuss it with him. They'd reached a truce of sorts, a place where his interests were being served as much as hers. After the night she'd demanded he please her, she was afraid of forcing him to bend to her will again.

Humor tugged at her. Imagine that, a Daughter giving a man his head out of fear of his adverse reaction to a more constricting hold.

George slapped a folder closed and shoved it aside. "You're

smiling a lot today."

Sigrid pretended interest in the graph estimating the ethnicity of one of the DNA samples. "I had a good weekend."

"With Will?"

"Who else?" She glanced at him and arched a teasing eyebrow. "These results won't analyze themselves."

He laughed, creasing his thinner face into a smile. "Ok, ok, you're the boss. I just... You seem really happy lately."

"I am."

Her happiness shouldn't have surprised her, but did. Before Will had stolen those kisses from her, she'd been at loose ends, bored, restless. He'd provided a small portion of the adventure she'd needed to jolt her out of a rut. More, he filled her life, easing the loneliness she hadn't even been aware of carrying.

"You're really going to fight another Daughter over him?" George asked.

"You heard about that?"

"Everybody has." He pushed through the short pile of folders resting between them and selected one. "I hope you kick her ass."

His words startled a laugh out of her. "I plan on doing so."

"See that you do. I've just gotten used to this side of you."

They settled back down to work. Sigrid set the results she'd been working on aside. The ethnicity was wrong, even accounting for statistical variations and the perils inherent to the methodologies used to estimate it. Too much Southeast African, not enough Near Eastern. She'd expect at least a three-quarter estimate of the latter ethnicity regardless of any other factor.

The next folder she snagged was for Jaran, a Daughter she knew by reputation only. Jaran had been decidedly African in origin, sub-Saharan, if Sigrid recalled correctly, a Daughter of a line that had been in Africa for at least three generations prior to her birth. For the sake of thoroughness, every set of results had to be checked. She flipped open the folder, sifted through the pages, went straight to the ethnicity, and stared.

Nearly one hundred percent Near Eastern. That had to be a mistake.

"We need to rerun these tests," she told George.

He glanced over, used one finger to push paper off the folder label, and shrugged. "Can't. We only had a partial skeleton to work with there and it was brittle. Really old, I thought. We got just enough DNA out of a femur to run the tests we needed."

Sigrid's heart began to pound as the implications presented by ancient bones began to form in her mind. Age wasn't the only factor in a bone's deterioration. Acidity, moisture, heat, all could contribute to a bone's breakdown, but age was so important.

"Jaran was only about fifteen hundred years old when she died, and that was just before my birth," Sigrid said.

George's eyes widened. "So you didn't know her?"

"I knew of her. My mother used to tell stories of Jaran, of the battles she fought, of the number of enemies she killed before they took her down." Even back then, when the People were scattered and their enemies were fierce, news had a way of making it into the right ear. "She was a fierce warrior, one of our finest, but she was several generations removed from her Sister ancestress. Look."

Sigrid showed him the ethnicity results and explained Jaran's heritage, or what she knew of it. "We can probably confirm some of her ancestry with Robert, or by interviewing her descendants."

"Yeah, we should look into that." George crossed one arm over his chest, propped the other elbow on it, and rubbed a hand over his mouth. "There must've been a mix-up somewhere. Either the samples or the results were mislabeled."

"Or the remains themselves were mixed up." Sigrid glanced at the files in front of them. "Do you remember running across results that would've approximated Jaran's ethnicity or otherwise matched her?"

"No, but we haven't tested all the museum's remains yet."

"And we still have results to sort through." Sigrid huffed out a sigh and eyed the folders scattered across the workbench. "Ok, let's start with what's in front of us."

They divided the remaining fifteen files between them and flipped through each one for the ethnicity report, the best way they had of determining which results belonged to Jaran. None matched, so they went to the workroom housing all of the remains from the museum and checked labels, sorted onto metal shelves running the length of the room.

George located the box labeled "Jaran: Ganenda: ca. 732 BCE - 766 CE" and placed it on the small table near the room's entrance, the only empty workspace in the room.

Sigrid opened the box and examined the few bones comprising the remains mislabeled as Jaran's. Age had painted a patina on the bones' surfaces, staining them brown like an old sepia toned photograph. A chill ran down Sigrid's spine. Could these be the remains of a Sister, or of a first generation Daughter? Was that even possible?

She retrieved archival gloves from the pocket of her lab coat, tugged them on, and lifted the femur from the Styrofoam cushioning it from further damage.

"What is it?" George asked.

She glanced at him, startled. She'd almost forgotten he was there. "What is what?"

"You got this funny look on your face."

"I don't know why."

She shook the lie away. Yes, she did, and he deserved to hear what she was beginning to suspect. How to tell him, though?

She carefully placed the femur back into its space and closed the lid. "I want these remains retested."

"But—"

Sigrid held a hand up, cutting George off in mid protest. "I know you said you've already extracted what you could. Try again. Find a way."

His mouth slammed shut and his lips pressed together into a thin line. "Ok. I'll see what I can dig up."

"In the meantime, let's concentrate on getting the rest of the museum's remains tested. We need to figure out which box contains the correct label for these bones, in case it contains additional information." She placed a protective hand over the box, patted it gently. "I think we may have found another Sister."

George's eyes went round in his face and he huffed out a laugh. "Holy shit."

"My thoughts exactly," she said, and spent the remainder of the workday helping him and the rest of their team collect and test samples.

Fourteen

Over the next few days, Will scrambled to fulfill every obligation he'd undertaken. He began by wrangling his sister into helping find housing for the newest residents of Tellowee, something she was in a better position to do given her front-end work at The Omega. As the head waitress and the assistant manager, she knew who was coming and going as well as Will did, and kept her ear to the ground for the undercurrents of town gossip, a habit she could put to good use now.

Together, Will and Casey hashed out wording for a help wanted flyer to be posted on the bulletin board nailed to the building's exterior, next to the entrance. While they were at it, they crafted a want ad for the local paper, a Plan B in case nobody in Tellowee needed a job. Hiring outside of the People was risky at best, especially when so many unfamiliar Daughters were streaming into town from parts of the world where Western culture was an unknown. The last thing he needed was for a local man to hit on a Daughter and end up dead, or worse, married to her in the way of the People.

Rebecca would have a field day explaining that one to the man's family.

Within a day of posting the flier, a couple of out of town Daughters applied for positions. Will left interviewing to Casey, with the permanent staff's input on a part-time bartender and another part-time cook, while Will took a day rummaging through Robert's research files and catching himself up on the status of the most important tasks.

By the end of the week, he was beat. Sigrid came in to The Omega every night like clockwork and stayed for an hour between the end of her workday and the beginning of her training. He snuck in kisses where he could and even managed half a dance with her before a squabble at the other end of the bar called him away.

Friggin' Daughters.

After that, he made sure Casey passed out a list of The Omega's rules to every newcomer, the last one of which emphatically stated, "Disobedience of any rule will result in expulsion and possible banishment."

On Friday night, he geared himself up for a hectic night on the floor. Casey had already hired four new staff members, two for the floor, one for the bar, and one for the kitchen, and started training them. For the first time in a good, long while, Will would spend most of his night either covering for breaks or working the crowd, keeping peace and a weather eye on newcomers and old timers alike.

When Sigrid pushed her way to the bar around seven, The Omega was packed with a crowd more than double its usual size. She jerked her chin at Will, and they edged toward each other through the mass of folks in need of entertainment.

He wrapped her in a hug, more out of a need to hold her than anything, and pitched his voice over the noise of laughter and music and the basketball game playing on the TV. "You look tired."

"Mmm. You, too." She sighed and leaned her head against his chest. "Are you coming over tonight?"

Desire sifted through him so quickly, it stole his breath. "If you want me to."

"Yes." Her finger traced the logo embroidered on his polo, etching heat in random patterns along the skin underneath.

"Would you train with me in the morning?"

The question startled him. He pulled away enough to meet her gaze. "You want to train with me?"

"I need a sparring partner." Her fingers trailed up his neck, and she cupped his face. "And a kiss."

"Happy to oblige," he murmured, and touched his mouth to hers. She hummed low in her throat and melted into him, and the desire she'd sparked off with her innocent touch morphed into a raging flame of need.

"I see the rumors are true," a cold voice said, cutting right through the sensual heat.

Will froze, still wrapped around Sigrid. His mother. Shit.

Sigrid eased out of his embrace and turned, facing his mother with her chin held high. "Wilhelmina. How are you?"

"Pissed off." Wilhelmina's gaze flicked to Will and her eyes narrowed in the honeyed oval of her face. "Your grandmother said you were enamored of this Daughter. I had no idea you felt free to kiss her in public."

Will pinched the bridge of his nose. "For fuck's sake, Mom. I'm a grown man."

"My beloved son is never old enough to publicly kiss a woman who isn't his wife."

Will's father sidled up beside her and placed a hand on his wife's shoulder. "Next time, Willie, you park the car and I greet our son."

"Hey, Dad."

Will leaned around Sigrid and clasped his father's hand in a firm handshake. It was like shaking the hand of an older version of himself. Troy Corbin stood exactly two inches taller than his wife's five foot eight inches, and sported close-cropped, graying blond hair the same shade as his only son's. The same dimples creased their cheeks when they smiled and their shoulders carried the same athletic breadth. At fifty-six, Will's father was still an attractive man, and had an uncanny ability to rein in his hard-headed wife.

Will dropped his father's hand and stepped back. Not for the first time, he wished he shared that particular trait with his dad.

Wilhelmina cast her cold gaze on her husband. "You can't possibly approve of his alliance with a Daughter of Sigrid's reputation."

"Hey, now," Will said, only to be overridden by his father.

"Will's a grown man," Troy said mildly.

"That he may be, but he also belongs to one of the most well-positioned families among the People." Wilhelmina shrugged out of her down jacket and draped it over one arm. "Custom must be followed."

"Custom be hanged," Will gritted out, then lowered his voice. "I'm not going to argue about it in the middle of a crowded bar."

Sigrid half turned toward him. "Lunch tomorrow at my house. Will that suit as neutral ground?"

"Yes," Will said, at the same time his mother said, "No."

Troy smiled faintly at Sigrid. "Of course. What can we bring?"

"Just yourselves." She turned an equally cold gaze on Wilhelmina. "Another Daughter and I are meeting in restricted combat soon."

Will just barely hid a wince. He hadn't told his mom about that yet. She was going to skewer him as soon as she got him alone.

"I've already contacted my attorney to set aside a settlement for Will," Sigrid continued.

Wilhelmina's eyebrows shot up. "You expect to win against Chana Wolfbane?"

"I expect to win against all comers," Sigrid said evenly. "Except Will. The decision is ultimately his. I won't force him to commit to me outside of the relationship we now have."

Surprise shot through him, and it was all he could do to keep his expression blank, as if he'd already known the terms

148

Sigrid would demand of him should she win.

Troy's gaze met Will's. Something flashed in his father's eyes, and was gone before Will could pinpoint exactly what it had been.

Wilhelmina nodded. "Fair enough. We'll see you tomorrow, then."

"One o'clock. Will works late tonight." Sigrid bowed toward his parents, each in turn, then faced Will. "I'll see you after work."

"Sure." He brushed a kiss across her mouth, uncaring of his mother's disapproving tut. Damn it, a man had a right to kiss his woman at the end of a long week. "Let me know if you need anything."

She smiled and slipped away, and disappeared into the crowd.

Troy waggled his eyebrows at Will. "I've always liked her. She's got spirit."

"Troy!" Wilhelmina said, and he laughed and tugged her into a hug and kissed her disapproval away.

Will rolled his eyes, amused in spite of himself. "C'mon, Dad, knock it off."

Troy smacked a final kiss to his dazed wife's mouth and winked at his son. "We're going to try to track down your sister in this crowd, then we're off for home. Your mother wouldn't even let me stop by the house so we could unload our luggage. Came straight here from the airport in Atlanta."

"For crying out loud, Mom," Will muttered, and she stared down her nose at him until he relented and hugged her. "Be good," he murmured against her ear. "I like her."

He bit back what he really wanted to say, that since Sigrid had walked into The Omega, he'd suspected she was *the one*. The more time he spent with her, the more he believed it. His heart teetered on the edge of love, held back only by her reputation. He crossed his arms over his chest and watched his parents drift away. No, not by her reputation, but by her high-handedness, and by the newness of it all. Time would take care of one concern. They were spending every minute together that each of them could spare.

And her high-handedness seemed to be melting away piece by piece. Maybe she'd eventually soften to him. Maybe she'd even grow to love him, the way he longed to love her, whole heartedly, in at the deep end, always and forever.

Eric called Will's name, dragging his attention back to the job at hand, and Will went back to work, his hopes and dreams and worries carefully tucked away.

SIGRID WAS in a tizzy by the time Will's parents arrived just before one the next afternoon. Oh, she didn't show it, not overtly, but Will was beginning to know her. She'd resettled the floral arrangement she'd had delivered half a dozen times, even though she'd placed it dead center on the dining room table on the very first try. The enchiladas she'd thrown together had suffered the same fate once she'd slid them into a hot oven, and she'd made at least two circuits of her entire house, searching for possible flaws in a spotless home.

The umpteenth time she opened the oven door and rechecked the enchiladas, he sidled up behind her and nuzzled a kiss to her throat. "Relax. Everything's fine."

Sigrid sucked in a breath, one palm pressed to her flat stomach over the ivory colored blouse she wore. "I know."

"Then why are you so fussy today?" He turned her gently around and pulled her into his chest, soothing her with a hug and tiny kisses pressed to her eyes, the tip of her nose, the stubborn set of her chin. "I've never seen you this rattled before, not even the day you challenged Chana."

Sigrid's breath huffed out into his chest and her fingernails scratched his skin lightly through his shirt. "Challenging that upstart didn't rattle me."

"Yeah? Is that why you pounced on me that night when I

got here?"

"I did not pounce. I insisted. There's a difference."

Interest stirred in spite of the stern lecture he'd given his body that morning. *Behave, or else.* Last thing he needed was his dick running amok while his mom was sitting across the table from him. "You gonna insist again later?"

Her fingers fluttered against him. "This is no joking matter, Will. Your mother has the authority to..."

Her words petered out, underlined by a tinge of emotion he'd never heard in her voice. He tilted her chin up and studied the calm mask her face had fallen into, save for the slight tremor of her lower lip. "What're you afraid of?"

"Nothing."

"You said that too quickly. Look." He tucked her against his chest again and smoothed his hands slowly up and down her back. "Mom can say anything she wants, but she can't touch me. I control my own assets. Dad insisted."

"I'm not worried about the money, Will."

"No, I know you're not, but it's an issue."

"Not the biggest one."

Her voice was tight, sharp, and it startled him. "You're really afraid of her."

Sigrid was silent for a long time. The fire popped in the fireplace, a light rain started falling outside, pattering against the cedar shingles, and the oven timer buzzed a warning.

At last, she said, "I'm afraid for you."

He shook his head, baffled. "Why?"

"Because you could lose your family over this."

She stepped away from him, easily avoided his grappling attempt to hold onto her, and pivoted toward the kitchen. He took one step toward her. No way was he letting her get by without discussing her fears, justified or not.

The doorbell rang, interrupting his pursuit, and he bit back a curse. That was some great timing his parents had. He'd needed five minutes, just five more minutes to coax Sigrid out of her funk, but no. His dad always had to arrive right on the nose. Just when he was getting Sigrid to open up, too.

Will shoved his fingers through his hair as he stared at the door Sigrid had disappeared through, then stalked into the foyer and yanked the front door open. His parents were standing on the porch wearing their Sunday best under wool coats dusted with a light coating of rain.

Resigned, he stepped back and let them in. "Hey. Lunch is almost ready."

Troy sniffed once as he helped his wife shed her coat. "Smells good."

"Enchiladas." Will took his mother's coat and hung it on the coatrack by the door, then helped his dad juggle taking off his coat with holding the wine they'd brought. "We've got a fire going."

Wilhelmina jerked down the cuffs of the deep red blouse she wore, then smoothed a hand over the front of her knee-length, black wool skirt. "We?"

"Get over it," Will said mildly. "Come on in. We can sit in the living room."

A door swung open, Sigrid's heels tapped ever louder, then she appeared in the living room ahead of them, her expression as calm and unruffled as usual, though her skin was pale even for her. "Hello."

Troy held out the wine and his dimples flashed. "Thanks for having us."

Sigrid's smile was faint. "You're welcome here any time."

Will jumped in, half afraid the conversation would devolve into a litany of polite chitchat. "How was Wellington?"

Wilhelmina perched on one end of the couch placed facing the fire, her hands folded primly in her lap. "Lovely, as usual."

Troy sat down beside her and placed one hand over hers. "It's a lot warmer there than it is here."

"We've had a mild winter while y'all were off playing tourists." Will waited until Sigrid settled herself into the recliner, then sat on the ottoman in front of it, deliberately placing himself between her and his mother. "Only one snowfall, and it was just a couple of inches."

Troy dove into retelling a memory from his own childhood days spent romping up and down the local mountains through inches of ice and snow, but Wilhelmina turned a calculating gaze on Will.

Good. She needed to know he wasn't going to give in to her just because she didn't like the direction his heart leaned. Let her fuss. As long as he had Sigrid, he'd do what he damn well pleased.

Lunch went much more smoothly than Will could've hoped. His mother relented enough to indulge in a light spate of gossip with Sigrid about her and Troy's recent travels, some near other centers of the People. Will spoke only when he had to. Sometimes it paid to observe and listen, a trait he'd learned when he first started tending bar. No one among the People ever said exactly what they meant unless pushed, and this conversation was no different. Beneath the surface, his mom and Sigrid were testing each other, politely probing boundaries and stratagem.

Troy caught Will's gaze near the end of the meal and nodded subtly toward the living room, and Will nearly shouted his relief. Thank the Great Mother for college football.

Not long after, his mother set aside her napkin. "I believe we have some business to attend."

Will pushed back his chair and stood. "Dad and I can clear the table while y'all talk."

Sigrid arched an eyebrow at him. "You would willingly miss negotiating your own future?"

"It's not like you're drawing up a contract today." He leaned down and brushed a kiss across her cheek. "Besides, there's a game on."

She gifted him with a faint smile. "How did men ever survive without modern sports?"

"Pillaging," he said firmly, then lowered his voice and

whispered against her ear, "Stop worrying so much. Everything's going to be fine."

He pulled away before she could speak and leveled a stern stare on his mother. "Behave."

She tilted her chin to a regal angle. "I always do."

Troy coughed into his fist, barely hiding a laugh as Sigrid rose.

"We shan't be long," she said, then led his mother out of the dining room toward her office.

As soon as they were out of earshot, Troy said, "So she's the one, huh?"

Will scowled down at the china he was stacking. "Who said that?"

"You do, every time you look at her. I know that look, son. See it in the mirror every time I think about your mom."

Will glanced up. "Is it that obvious?"

"To me, yeah. To your mom?" Troy shrugged and lifted a stack of dirty plates. "She's blind where her beloved son is concerned."

"She needs to back off," Will gritted out.

"And let you decide on your own? When did a Daughter ever do that?"

Some of his frustration bled away under his dad's amusement. "You've got a point."

"She'll come around. You'll see."

That's what he was worried about, that she'd come around after it was too late to do him any good. Sigrid was right. If he wasn't careful, his relationship with her could drive a wedge between him and his mother, especially if Chana won and Will opted to pay the requisite fines rather than honor the challenge's outcome.

Chana seemed nice enough, but no way in Hell was he stupid enough to tie himself to a stranger. At least he knew Sigrid well enough to trust her.

He stopped stock still in the middle of pushing open the

kitchen door and his eyes slid closed. Fuck, how had that happened? Trust was only a tiny, fragile step away from love, and he wasn't ready yet, wasn't ready to tumble head over heels for a woman he wasn't certain could ever love him. Ok, so she was getting there quicker than he would've thought, but there was no guarantee she wouldn't turn tail and run. It wouldn't be the first time a Daughter abandoned a man rather than succumb to her tender heart. Probably wouldn't be the last either.

He continued on into the kitchen and shooed his dad into the living room to find a game, then cleaned up while he tried to talk some sense into his own too tender heart.

SIGRID CLOSED her office door, shutting out the men's voices echoing faintly through the house. She turned toward Will's mother and gestured toward the sitting area occupying one corner of the room. "Please, have a seat."

"Thank you." Wilhelmina perched on the edge of an overstuffed leather armchair the color of warm chocolate. "You're sleeping with my son."

Sigrid refused to let the sharp remark rankle. She took the chair opposite her oldest friend's daughter without a single hesitation in her actions. "He and I have a deepening relationship, yes."

"You're fucking him," Wilhelmina said bluntly. "Did you seduce him before or after approaching my mother for the right to court him?"

Sigrid crossed one leg over the other, deliberately icy in the face of the heat underlying Wilhelmina's words. "Your son approached me, but that isn't the issue here."

"The issue is the despoilment of my son."

Sigrid threw her head back and laughed, genuinely amused in spite of the threat Will's mother posed. "Will needed no despoiling, I assure you. He's quite capable of handling whatever situation arises."

Pride flashed briefly across Wilhelmina's expression, and was abruptly shuttered. "He's worthy of any woman he seeks."

"Does it bother you more that he chose me, or that he failed to ask permission first?" Sigrid slashed her hand through the air. "Let's cut to the chase. What remuneration do you want me to set aside for him?"

"Should you win against Chana," Wilhelmina said.

"*When* I win," Sigrid corrected. "And rest assured, Wilhelmina, I will win."

"Because you don't want to tarnish your unbroken chain of victories, or because you love him?"

Sigrid fixed her own expression into a cold, dispassionate mask. "Does it matter?"

"Perhaps not," Wilhelmina murmured. "Why did you challenge her?"

"She had the temerity to touch my property."

"And by property, you mean my son." Wilhelmina's mouth curled into a mocking sneer. "This from the woman who discards lovers so frequently, she can't remember their names."

"Will is the grandson of an old friend," Sigrid said, and hated the stiffness in her voice. "If not for that, I would've called Chana out then and there."

"Over such a trifling?" Wilhelmina clucked her tongue against the roof of her mouth. "You're getting soft in your old age, Sigrid, and over a mere mortal man."

"That man," Sigrid said, her words deadly soft, "is your son. I will not have you speak of him in such a manner."

Wilhelmina's eyebrows shot up. She sat back in the chair as a knowing smile tilted her lips. "You're in love with him, aren't you?"

Sigrid barely bit back a muttered curse. That was the second time in a week she'd been accused of loving Will. Was she so transparent that anyone could notice the softening of her heart? "He's a good man and a credit to your family."

"Which doesn't answer my question. Interesting."

Wilhelmina reclasped her hands in her lap and her gaze grew shrewd. "Half of your current holdings, one quarter upon a commitment, the other upon the birth of a healthy child, with a further penalty of twenty-five percent of the total should you forsake him."

Sigrid nodded once. "I'll consider your request."

"I'm sure you'll do more than consider it if you want him in your life." Wilhelmina stood, triumph etched into her posture. "He may think he holds all the cards, but I assure you, he does not."

With that, Wilhelmina strode out of the room, shutting the door quietly behind herself. Sigrid slumped into her chair and closed her eyes, her heart a thin flutter in her chest. By the Lady Ki, that had not gone well. And now Will, sweet Will with his soft kisses and passionate touch, Will with his wide open heart...

She was going to lose him.

Her hands trembled in her lap and sorrow rose so swiftly, she had no chance to staunch the tears it drew from her. Will gone, because she'd mishandled the initial interview with his mother, one of the few obstacles in their path. Stupid. Why had she let a single, An-cursed emotion show? Why hadn't she found a way to counter Wilhelmina's certainty?

Sigrid sucked in a ragged breath, snagged a tissue, and blotted her eyes, capturing the tears sliding down her cheeks before they could betray her emotions.

Fifteen

Early Monday morning, Sigrid walked across campus for her appointment with Rebecca Upton. Her team hadn't yet located the box containing the remains stored erroneously in the one that should've contained Jaran's skeleton, but they were making steady progress testing the many skeletal remains that had been stored at the IECS museum. The discovery of the correct box could occur at any moment, thus hopefully shedding light on the brittle bones of a possible Sister, *possible* being the operative word.

Sigrid jogged up the marble stairs fronting the main IECS office building and pulled the door open. In spite of her instinct's insistence and the test results she'd personally pored over for hours, too much uncertainty remained. Everything hinged on careful retesting and examining the label of the storage box the bones had originally been housed in. Patience, she cautioned herself, but her patience, usually in such abundant supply, was running perilously thin.

She was going to lose Will.

Sigrid swallowed the bleak thought as soon as it arose, just as she'd done the dozens of other times it had popped into her mind since his mother walked out of their meeting on Saturday afternoon. Oh, Wilhelmina had been polite enough during the remainder of her and her husband's visit, gracious even, but her smug triumph had cast a pall over the gathering.

It should've been a happy time, one of celebration and triumph of a different sort all together, that of two families intermingling through the union of two of its most respected members.

Sigrid shook disappointment away and marched into the director's outer office with her head held high and her confidence firmly in place. There were more important events to consider now, ones with much larger ramifications on the People's future than the trifling prospect of a lone Daughter losing a man's affections.

Director Upton's receptionist buzzed Sigrid through, and Sigrid walked in and shut the door behind herself.

Rebecca was sitting ramrod straight behind her desk, not a hair out of place. She glanced up as Sigrid approached and proffered a tired smile. "I hope you have good news."

"I wish I could say I did." Sigrid perched on the edge of a chair in front of Rebecca's desk, set her briefcase on the chair next to her, and opened it. "I have a report on our latest findings for you."

Rebecca waved a hand at her. "Summarize, please. I'm not sure I can decipher all the science behind your work this early on a Monday morning."

Sigrid tugged out a copy of the report and passed it across Rebecca's desk. "We've been running a variety of tests on the known Bones of the Just and using those as a measuring stick for tests on other remains."

"And?"

"We may have found the remains of two other Sisters." Sigrid held up her hands, nipping Rebecca's enthusiasm in the bud. "The tests we're using are problematic. It's not just about DNA. We know all the remains are of direct descendants of the Sisters, if not the Sisters themselves, thanks to the miracle of mitochondrial DNA."

Rebecca sat back in her chair and steepled her fingers

together under her chin. "I thought testing mitochondrial DNA was a relatively simple and reliable procedure."

"It is. That's not the problem we're running into." Briefly, Sigrid explained their shift to using ethnicity estimates and the problems inherent to the methodology. "George introduced the idea and discovered, as we would've expected, that the Sisters ethnicity was nearly one hundred percent Near Eastern, though there were slight variations as to the exact percentage from Sister to Sister."

"And the two sets of remains you believe may also be Sisters?"

"The ethnicity is a match, and the mitochondrial DNA does support their being of the People, but as to certainty?" Sigrid rolled her shoulders under the ivory suit jacket she wore. "Perhaps with other documentation, we could be more certain, but the science isn't there yet."

Rebecca dropped her hands and her gaze drifted away. "If it's a matter of more staff or equipment..."

"I wish it were that simple. We're continuing our work, sifting through results as soon as they're available, and George discovers a new angle almost every day, but this is what we have to work with for the moment." Sigrid threaded her fingers together and rested them in her lap. "How's Robert?"

Rebecca's gaze snapped back to Sigrid's. "Fine," she said evenly.

"Will told me he was ill." Sigrid held up a hand, forestalling Rebecca's next comment. "He only told me that, nothing more, and I didn't press."

"I've never known you to back down when you wanted to know something."

Unaccountably, heat rose in Sigrid's cheeks. She coughed lightly into her fist, clearing her throat. "It seemed like a sensitive matter."

"Sensitive?" Rebecca huffed out a short laugh. "Moira told me you were dating Will, but I didn't realize matters were so serious. Does Wilhelmina know?"

Sigrid barely stifled a flinch. "Yes."

"That must not have gone well."

It hadn't, but nothing could be done about it now. "We'll deal with it in due time."

"We," Rebecca murmured, then shook her head, a bemused expression gracing her delicate features.

Sigrid interrupted, half afraid of Rebecca's next words. "One more thing. We have the results back on the blood of the Woman with No Face."

Rebecca leaned forward, eyebrows arched. "And?"

"She's old, Director, very old, and probably born before the Sisters moved the People out of the Levant." Sigrid allowed a small smile to curve her lips. "I can explain the science for you, if you like."

Rebecca's laughter held genuine humor. "Thank you for the update, but I'll pass on the science. Please let me know if I can aid your efforts in any way."

Sigrid rose and bowed, thanked Rebecca, and left, not certain whether the director had aimed her offer of help toward the problems surrounding identifying the Bones of the Just, or the problems surrounding Sigrid's burgeoning relationship with Will.

WILL WOKE UP alone in Sigrid's bed a little before noon. After the dismal meeting with his mother, it hadn't taken much persuading for him to stay with Sigrid beyond the weekend. Yeah, so he'd promised to give it time and not rush into anything, and he'd fully intended to.

Until Sigrid slipped out of her office Saturday afternoon behind his mother, her nose a little too red for the room's warmth.

She'd been crying.

He rolled over onto Sigrid's side of the bed and bunched

her pillow up under his head. The light, floral scent of her shampoo drifted to him and, predictably, his morning woody went from rock hard to rocketing to get off.

Already, he was addicted to her.

He huffed out a humorless laugh into her pillow. Meanwhile, she'd gone cold on him again. It had taken all his patience to coax her into cuddling with him Saturday night after he came to bed. Even half asleep, she'd resisted. Frustration had pushed him into settling the matter the old fashioned way, with a mind-numbing, heart-thumping, melt your bones inside and out kiss, and it had worked, thank Ki.

She'd let him curl around her through the rest of the night without another objection, but last night, she'd reverted to Ice Queen and tried to push him away again. In between, during the hours he'd spent working on one project or another, she'd tagged along and helped out where she could, sure, but she was silent, always watching, like something evil was about to strike and only her constant vigilance kept it at bay.

Damn it, he was getting tired of having to thaw her out.

And the exhibition was Friday night, less than a week away. She needed to focus, needed to train. He'd help her how and where he could, but he needed something, too. Reciprocation, if nothing else. Mutual affection and support. *Something.* Was that too much to ask?

He pushed his worry away and tried to relax, and dozed fitfully until his alarm went off, signaling the beginning of his day. Sigrid was in meetings all day, so he met Ethan for a weight lifting session at the IECS gym, then ordered a quick lunch from Tellowee's only restaurant, a meat and three that doubled as a deli, and took it to Robert's office for a couple of hours of work there.

Will settled down in Robert's chair, and while he ate, he listened to the voice messages that had accumulated since he'd checked the answering machine the day after Robert's hospitalization. Some of it was personal. Will skipped those, leaving them for Robert to handle, and jotted notes for the ones he needed to return.

One call was from a genealogist in Connecticut that Robert had asked to dig into James Terhune's ancestry. Rhonda Bowman was the wife of a Son, and a respected colleague from Robert's days as a professor of history. Her message was brief and to the point: *Found something important. Please call asap.*

Will finished his lunch, cleared his trash, and took a quick trip to the men's room to clean up. As soon as he sat down at Robert's desk again, he picked up the phone's handset and dialed Rhonda. She answered with a terse, "Hello."

"Mrs. Bowman, this is Will Corbin. I'm an associate of Robert Upton's at the Institute for Early Cultural Studies in Tellowee, Georgia."

A long pause followed. "I expected Robert to return my call."

"He's out of the office for a while." No need to say why. If Robert wanted her to know, he'd tell her. "I'm taking care of his current research projects until his return. You're working on James Terhune's ancestry?"

"Yes." Just when Will thought he was going to have to prompt her, she continued in her sharp, Yankee accent. "He's of the People through his mother's line, which confirms the DNA tests Robert sent me. My research indicates he's descended from the line of Abragni."

Excitement skipped through Will. He'd gotten to know James pretty well since the archaic language expert's arrival in Tellowee a few months back, and liked him. To learn the other man was a cousin, however distant? Amazing.

"Do you know which line?" he asked.

"Yes, I—" The line crackled and popped, and Rhonda sighed. "It's storming here. I'll mail copies of the research to Robert. If you have any questions, shoot me an email."

"Sure. Thanks for the help."

Will hung up and sat back in the chair. It creaked and

bounced under his shifting weight, reminding him of the many hours he'd spent helping Robert in the decade and a half since his apprenticeship, and of his own obligations to the People.

James Terhune was a cousin.

Will grinned and logged into Robert's desktop computer. An email to James wouldn't take long, then Will could hunker down with the other research he'd planned to oversee today, much of it related to the tests Sigrid and George were running. He needed to track down the living descendants of a Daughter named Jaran, among others, but for now, he intended to connect with a newly found relative and share the good news.

Sixteen

Sigrid trained harder than ever after the run in with Will's mother, spurred by an icy fear flowing through her veins. Every moment not spent at work or with Will was bent to the singular task of defeating Chana Wolfbane in their upcoming match. Anything less was unthinkable.

So Sigrid trained, and she trained some more, both at home and at the gym on the IECS campus. There, she tested her skill against other Daughters seeking the same. So ruthless was she that few of the younger, less experienced Daughters sought her out for a bout.

Rumors spread quickly. The Deathknell tolled for any soul foolish enough to brave facing Sigrid in combat.

Let them talk. Let their words reach the ear of her opponents. Let *them* fear her wrath.

The day before the exhibition, Sigrid sat in her office studying the results of yet more tests. They were getting close to an answer. She could feel it in her bones. Three Sisters known, two more possible, and dozens of lineages solidified through painstaking genealogical research coupled with the judicious use of science.

Soon, the Bones of the Just would rest in a Sanctuary of the People's choosing, and they could then destroy their enemy and forever after be free of the shadow of An's curse.

Blessed be Ki.

A soft tap hit her door, then George poked his head inside, his skin ashen under the untidy mop of his hair. "I have to leave."

Sigrid set aside the file she was studying and stood. "What's wrong?"

"My parents." His hand tightened on the doorknob and if anything, he skin went even paler. "There's been an accident. My sister called. I need to get home."

She skirted her desk, then took his cold hands in hers and led him to a chair in front of her desk. "Have you made travel arrangements?"

"Yeah. No." He shook his head and his eyes squeezed shut. "My sister did. I'm booked on the earliest flight she could find."

"Would you like me to drive you to the airport?"

"James is. I just..." He shrugged and dropped his head back, eyes open and brimming with unshed tears. "Dad's in surgery. Internal bleeding. Mom's got a couple of broken bones. Some idiot ran a stoplight. Dad swerved, but—"

"Shush," she said gently. "You'll worry yourself to death thinking about something over which you have no control. I'll escort you to your apartment and help you pack."

He huffed out a short laugh and finally looked at her, sniffing through the tears. "Trust a Daughter to cut through to the practical."

"After centuries of living, one learns that practical is the most efficient course." She rubbed his hands between her own, warming them. "What time is your flight?"

"Ten tonight."

"Then we'd best get you to your apartment. You'll need plenty of time for the drive and airport security. Do you have enough money?"

His eyes widened and a laugh sputtered out of him, morphing into a deep belly laugh.

She arched an eyebrow. "What?"

"You," he gasped out. Tears trickled down his cheeks and he swiped them away, then inhaled a deep, cleansing breath and grinned at her. "You sound like my mom, asking if I need money."

"Since I'm a mother, I can hardly take offense for acting like one."

"I guess not." He flipped his hands over in hers and held them gently. "Thanks. I guess I needed somebody to talk me down."

"It's what I'm here for." Among other things. "Now, go make sure your computer is shut down in your office and gather up any personal items you need for the journey. I have a phone call to make before escorting you to your apartment."

"You don't have to do that."

"Yes, I do." And not only out of duty, though she could hardly tell him that. She cupped his baby face in her hands and brushed the last remnants of his tears off his cheeks. "You must have faith, George. All will be as it should."

He nodded once, then she stepped away from him and watched him hustle out of her office. As soon as he was safely away, she sat down behind her desk and pulled up a private database of contact information for members of the People. A certain young Daughter needed to know what was going on in George's life. George wouldn't call his heart's love. He'd made it clear during his conversation with Sigrid that he intended to honor Andrea's wishes and leave her alone.

Sigrid had no such qualms.

She located Andrea's number and placed the call, certain this was one battle she could easily win.

WILL SPENT the week leading up to the exhibition putting out fires on a variety of fronts. On Tuesday, Eric called in sick with the flu, sounding so bad Will had pity on him and told him to take as much time as he needed. Eric promised to come in as soon as he could, but his absence left a hole Will had a hard time filling. He ended up tending bar himself around finalizing the roster for Friday's exhibition and juggling the extra duties piled onto his plate.

On Wednesday, half a dozen non-local Daughters approached him individually and demanded to be put on the roster for the upcoming competition. Will called Rebecca, who suggested a blind draw for some of the matches, and offered to organize the setup of an extra set of mats to accommodate the additional fighters.

Robert had finally been dismissed from the hospital, but he was confined to home, so Will was still covering for the older man. Research was slowly trickling in. Soon, Jaran's descendants would be found and their DNA samples matched against the bones Sigrid had told him about. Tired as he was, even he was anxious to know who the bones really belonged to.

And he was tired. His days were getting longer, his sleep shorter, and the few minutes he could spare every day for Sigrid weren't nearly enough to satisfy him.

The crush he'd had on her was gradually morphing into something deeper. He was doing everything he could to slow down the leap into love, but none of his efforts pulled him away from the brink he was teetering on.

On Thursday, he spared a precious half hour in his office for re-ordering supplies. The extra crowds drew heavily on The Omega's stockpile of craft beer and hard liquor. Oddly enough, the crowd's favorite had shifted from chicken tenders and fries to fish sticks and homemade potato chips. The kitchen was going through a twenty pound bag of russet potatoes every day, and running out well short of closing.

Maybe he needed to hire someone just for prep work.

Will threw down his pen, leaned back in his chair, and scrubbed his palms over his face. Fatigue ate at him, wearing him down under the mountain of *stuff* he still had to do.

Replenishment drinks and high carb snacks for the exhibition, sorting out the steady influx of visitors, his mother and her stubborn high-handedness, and for fuck's sake, he still had to man the floor tonight.

He closed his eyes against the fluorescent lights glowing overhead. Five minutes of rest, just five minutes to not worry about anything, or plan, or juggle, or think.

A knock hit the door, startling him awake. He rubbed a hand over his face, blinked sleep out of his eyes, and said, "Yeah?"

Casey poked her head in and scrunched her face into a grimace. "You look like crap, big brother."

"Just what I needed to hear. What's up?"

"We've got a Daughter out here who says she has a score to settle with another Daughter. They want to have a juried fight tomorrow night, with a high-ranking Daughter as the final judge."

Will bit back a curse. "Tell her I'll be out in a minute."

"Yeah, sure." Casey eased all the way into his office and shut the door behind herself, then leaned back against it. "Mom's livid about Sigrid."

"Tell me something I don't know."

"She's gone quiet, like she's planning something."

Will propped his elbows on the edge of his desk and dropped his head into his hands. Damn it, why couldn't she just accept this one thing? He'd never asked anything of her, and always done what she'd asked. Take over the bar at sixteen so she and Dad could take off? No problem. Set aside college for a couple of years so Casey could finish high school here instead of on the road? Will had it covered.

All his life, he'd done exactly what his mother had wanted. He'd toed the line so hard, his shoes were permanently worn at the tips. Now when he was on the verge of finding love, when his relationship with Sigrid held so much potential, why couldn't his mom just back off and let him figure it out on his own?

A soft hand stroked down his back, and Casey said, "Are

you really sure you want to defy her?"

Will huffed out a laugh, shook his head. "She can't run my life forever."

"No, but she can make it hard on you. You know what she's like. She has to have her way, and she's too hardheaded to forgive somebody who doesn't bend to her will."

"She'll have to if she wants to see me again."

"Will, c'mon. Don't say that."

A thin thread of fear wove through Casey's words, and he understood without her saying exactly what would happen if their mother couldn't accept his decisions where Sigrid was concerned. Wilhelmina would withdraw her support of Will, or possibly disown him, and in the doing, she'd forbid the rest of the family from having any contact with him. He'd be isolated, a pariah. The People would turn their backs on him, and on Sigrid, too, for aiding his defiance. There'd be no safe haven for them, nowhere they could go to escape his mother's judgment.

Oh, she'd suffer, too. Abandoning a Son came at a high price, but if she was mad enough, if she felt it was the only way to bring him to heel, she'd cut him off without a single hesitation, leaving him friendless, jobless, homeless. He had enough stashed away to survive for decades, but all the money in the world wouldn't fix the severed ties to his family and friends.

Will stood and pulled his sister into a hug, tucked her head under his chin, and smoothed his hands up and down her back. "Don't worry, Case. It'll be ok."

"You can't know that," she said into his chest, her words so soft they were barely audible.

"I can. Don't worry, ok? You're still my kid sister, no matter what."

She laughed and tightened her arms around him, and they stood that way for a long time, clinging to the moment as if it were their last.

FRIDAY AFTERNOON, Will closed The Omega at two and shooed everybody out. He left Casey to oversee cleanup and headed over to Tellowee's high school, located on the IECS campus. School was still in session when he arrived, so he tracked down a gym teacher and borrowed a handful of teenagers to help him set up.

There really wasn't much left to do. Caterers were bringing in finger foods at five. Two of the students, Dierdre Bellegarde and her step-sister Amelia Terhune, James's daughter, volunteered to retrieve the extra Gatorade and bottled water he'd ordered for the event from the bowels of the Archives. A third, Johnny Linton, went with them as the driver and, as he put it, the muscle, and the trio jogged out of the gym laughing and cutting up.

Will shook his head and directed the other students to help him pull out bleachers and set up mats. So many adults had wanted to participate, they'd had to move the youngest kids' portion to the next day, before the second round of the competitive matches. Only teenagers and up would compete that night, the teens in a group of their own, including some out-of-towners who'd shown up with older family members.

Most of the adults had randomly been assigned partners. Only a few, like Sigrid and Chana, were fighting specific challenges. Interestingly enough, those included a bout between Rebecca and Lukas Alexiou. She hadn't said what the challenge was over when she'd asked him to include it in the night's activities, and he'd respected her privacy. It would come out before the fight anyway.

In the meantime, gossip would fly once the attendees spotted that particular challenge on the posters he'd pinned to a prominent location inside the gym.

He hadn't seen Sigrid since he'd dropped into her bed last night and curled himself around her sleeping form. She'd been long gone when he awoke a mere five hours later. Her pillow had carried her scent, but none of her warmth.

A pang touched his heart. He rubbed a palm against it and scowled at the night's lineup, neatly printed by a local copy shop on a glossy, movie poster sized sheet of paper. Damn it, he missed her. He missed talking to her and holding her, and he missed being inside her. At the rate events were unfolding, they wouldn't be able to have sex again until after whatever was steamrolling toward them had passed, and maybe not then.

That was unacceptable.

He dropped his hand and pivoted around, heading toward the locker room. She would by Ki come out and talk to him before the match. A kiss wouldn't kill her, would it? And maybe it'd rattle Chana a little, knowing he favored another.

The memory of the confrontation between her and Sigrid flitted through his mind, and he winced. Yeah, probably not. That one was a little too sure of herself, thanks to his meddling grandmother.

One day, the women in his family would learn to keep their noses out of his business.

He rubbed a hand over his nape, squeezed the back of his neck. Maybe on a cold day in hell. Blessed Ki, when had his life gotten so complicated?

He jogged down the short flight of stairs toward the women's locker room, strode along the short hallway, and banged a fist into the closed door separating him from his lover. Coaxing Sigrid into a kiss would be simple enough, at least, and then he could retreat to the sidelines and pray like hell she won so he'd have one less thing to worry about.

Seventeen

Sigrid stood on the sidelines watching the fiercely competitive matches taking place on two large mats placed on opposite ends of the gym floor.

Will had snuck a kiss from her while she was dressing, though she'd sworn to avoid him before the match. His presence was a distraction she could ill afford, yet when he'd banged on the locker room door and shouted for her, she'd obeyed his summons like a schoolgirl in the first throes of a crush. As soon as she'd appeared in the doorway, he'd dragged her into the hall, pinned her to the painted concrete block wall, and kissed her senseless right there where any passerby could witness her defeat.

Even now, her lips tingled from his touch, and she was keenly aware of his presence some twenty feet distant. His gaze rested on the match taking place closest to him, yet his attention seemed elsewhere, as if he were pondering a matter of great import.

Two guesses as to what.

A woman settled into the spot beside Sigrid. She glanced out of the corners of her eyes, scarcely moving her head, and sighed. Chana. Wasn't their forthcoming match soon enough for another confrontation?

"You have no family here?" Chana asked.

"In the bleachers," Sigrid said. "Should you wish your companions to remain on the floor, it can be arranged."

"I prefer them far away. A Daughter fights her battles alone, yes?"

Sigrid grunted. No matter how far the People scattered across the ends of the Earth, or how varied their practices, some things remained the same.

Chana jerked her chin at Will. "I see the way he looks at you. His heart will not stay my hand, or temper my blows."

"Nor will it mine." Sigrid shifted toward Chana, one eyebrow arched. "Why do you pursue him, knowing his heart lies elsewhere?"

Something flashed across Chana's expression, a moment of vulnerability, perhaps, and was gone just as quickly. She ducked her head, inhaled a long breath, and when she raised her head, her expression was hard and resolute. "He reminds me of someone I knew long, long ago."

An understandable reason, even under the circumstances. A Daughter's long life brought many loves, if she was lucky, though not every beloved mate could break a Daughter's curse. Only one special man could do that, the one a Daughter could trust and love above all others.

Sigrid's gaze drifted to Will. He stood exactly where he had since she'd walked out of the locker room and onto the gym floor, still as a statue with his arms crossed over his wide chest and his lower lip pinched between thumb and forefinger. Was he that special man for her? Could he break her curse, give her the Son she'd only thought of in her most secret dreams? Would he be the man she would live out the remainder of her natural life with, side by side, in a bond so eternal, even An's curse could never stand between them?

For a moment, she yearned. What would it be like to have that all-consuming connection with Will, to love him so much, she gave everything to him?

A whistle blew, signaling the end of a match, and Sigrid

snapped out of her reverie. She had sworn to never submit to a man, to serve the People always as an immortal, until the day their enemies were defeated and the curse was broken by the fulfillment of the Prophecy, leaving them free to love as they chose.

That day could be soon, her heart murmured, and she cut it off, snuffing every emotion as if they were lights glowing within her. She would give Will what she could, though she could never give him what he wanted. To do that, she must win, and to win, she must be cold, ruthless, unfeeling.

As she had once been to Will.

She shoved the small pang away and focused on the Daughters streaming on and off the floor, preparing for another bout. "Have you decided on a weapon?"

"A baston made of rattan," Chana said promptly, and her dark eyes cut sideways toward Sigrid. "I have no wish to permanently maim you."

Sigrid nodded, oddly relieved. The baston was a simple stick a little more than two feet in length, and one of the first weapons modern children of the People learned to use. Deadly enough for combat in the right hands, but lacking the sharp edges of many of the People's other favored weapons. She'd picked up stick fighting at a more advanced age, but it had become, like swordplay, so ingrained she could fight blindfolded. Sticks weren't her best weapon, no; swords were and always had been. Still, the baston was a fitting weapon. It would be a good fight, well-matched, and in the end, the best Daughter would win the prize.

Sweet Will.

"Nor I you," she said at last.

She stood next to Chana in a companionable silence, her blood thrumming with purpose and determination, and a hope she could scarcely acknowledge.

THEIRS WAS the second challenge match scheduled, succeeding a bout between Ethan Phillips and Levi Ewart over a slight of honor involving Levi's mortal wife. The two Sons, one of the line of Abragni, the other of the line of Bagda and a distant cousin to Sigrid, ruthlessly exchanged blows using their fists or open hands, or any other body part positioned within striking distance of the other Son.

The match was refereed by a neutral judge, one not directly related to either party. The men were evenly matched, tall and strong and creative in their attacks and defenses, and equally determined to win. At two points each and nearly twenty minutes into the challenge, both stood ready for more.

It might have stayed that way if Ethan hadn't lost his balance at the end of a half-roundhouse kick aimed at Levi's knee. Levi reacted quickly, pushing Ethan down in the direction of his stumble, then followed him onto the mat. A single fist rose and fell, striking a hard blow to Ethan's jaw, then to his chest. The judge blew her whistle and counted the point for Levi, ending the match.

The younger Son levered himself upright and said, his voice hard, "Stay away from my wife, Phillips."

He stalked off toward the locker room as the crowd's murmurs slowly increased in volume and Ethan rolled over and pushed himself off the mat, looking not one whit defeated by the challenge's outcome.

A handful of teenagers rushed onto the floor and scrubbed the mat down, then another judge stepped forward and beckoned toward Sigrid and Chana, summoning them for their match. The judge, an immortal Daughter whose nearly black, almond shaped eyes glinted impassively in the olive-toned rectangle of her face, was a newcomer chosen by Rebecca as a neutral party of a line other than Sigrid's or Chana's.

Sigrid knew her by sight only, and cared not at all who the woman was. Any judge was better than the alternative, traditionally the highest ranking Daughter at hand, usually a

Councilmember. As far as she knew, the only Councilmember nearby was Will's grandmother.

Rebecca had had enough mercy to eschew tradition in favor of a fair fight, thank Ki.

The judge held two bastons at her side, one in each hand. "Face each other and repeat the challenge."

Sigrid stepped onto the mat to the judge's right and waited for Chana to take the opposite position before speaking. "I challenge you, Chana Wolfbane, Daughter of Pari Bakhshesh, of the line of Eleni, for your untoward interest in my lover Will Corbin, beloved Son of Wilhelmina the Fierce, grandson of Anya Bloodletter, the embodiment of Abragni and a member of the Council of Seven."

Chana's eyes rounded slightly, as if she were surprised by the mention of Will's status among the People, but she merely said, "I accept your challenge, Sigrid Deathknell, Daughter of Glyvyn the Ice Warrior, of the line of Bagda."

The judge handed each a baston. "Three points scored with the baston to the front torso from waist to shoulder. No other hits will be scored. Test your weapons."

Sigrid took the baston offered her and inspected it from one rounded tip to the other. Rattan was a lightweight, flexible wood when cut correctly. This baston appeared to be newly made, though it had to be older as the People had stopped purchasing rattan bastons a decade back due to issues with unsustainable harvests. No cracks appeared in the baston's gleaming, unmarked finish, and it felt solid under the firm fist she slid down its length, testing for weaknesses. She gripped one end and swung it across her body, then up in a sideways slash. A satisfying whistle accompanied the swings, and Sigrid grunted. Good enough.

Across from her, Chana finished testing her baston with a circling swing over her head followed by a downward cut. She nodded at the judge, then faced Sigrid squarely, her chin high and her shoulders squared.

"Ready?" the judge asked, and at their nods she stepped off

the mat and said, "Begin."

Sigrid stepped to her left and in, slightly closing the distance between her and her opponent as Chana mirrored the action. Slowly they circled the mat, each step bringing them closer, their eyes focused not on each other's faces, but on the torso, taking in every action the other made, waiting for the first strike.

Chana led there. When they were five feet apart, barely within striking distance, she leapt forward and stabbed the end of her baston at Sigrid's heart. Sigrid swept her baston up and over, easily countering Chana's thrust, then swung it up under Chana's striking arm. Chana hopped back, evading the blow, and the fight was on in a flurry of attacks and counterattacks around the mat.

Sigrid's focus narrowed to the woman in front of her. The restless stirrings in the crowd faded away, their quiet commentary silenced, and the tether strung between her and Will muted to a bare whisper of awareness in her mind. She lost track of time and of the room, and left only enough outside attention for the judge hovering on the mat's periphery.

Her body moved smoothly, efficiently deflecting each blow, or accepting it if doing so lead to an opening in Chana's defenses. She left offensive strikes to instinct, thrusting when Chana overreached or slashing when her opponent's step seemed hesitant, never allowing her own defenses to falter, ignoring the bruises accumulating up and down her body, and the pain.

If you cannot kill quickly, her mother had counseled, *wear your opponent down. You have the stamina of an immortal Daughter in your blood, passed down through generations from one of the greatest warriors of our People. Use it well, Daughter.*

Sigrid always had, in battle when her life and livelihood were at stake, and now, when her future hung in the balance. One mistake could lose the day. One lapse of judgment and victory could go to Chana.

Her heart trembled in her chest. She clamped down on it and forced her attention where it belonged, on the baston Chana wielded so gracefully. It snaked toward Sigrid, aiming for her ribcage, and Sigrid shoved it away with a sweep of her left hand.

Sneaky little Persian. Perhaps a change of tactics was in order.

Sigrid eased away from Chana, forcing the other woman to follow her, and circled around the mat, waiting for an opening. It came soon enough. Sigrid had been sidling to her left, allowing Chana to become complacent. Chana executed a rapid series of punishing blows aimed at Sigrid's left rib cage. Sigrid deflected them, her breath a shallow pant in her lungs, then slid to the right and cracked her baston into Chana's left thigh, just above the knee.

Chana's leg crumpled, throwing her off balance. Sigrid swept her foot under the injured leg, helping her opponent down, then slid the end of her baston under Chana's scrambling defense and tapped her in the sternum.

The judge said, "Point, Sigrid," even as Chana caught Sigrid's free arm, lifted her uninjured leg into Sigrid's stomach, and used Sigrid's slight forward momentum to tumble her into a somersault over Chana's head. Sigrid's hands slapped down onto the mat, automatically cushioning her fall. Chana rolled into a handstand following Sigrid's tumble, landed on one leg, and tapped her own baston against Sigrid's ribcage just above the waist, evading Sigrid's defensive swipes.

The judge called, "Point, Chana. One each."

Pain blossomed around the point of the blow. Sigrid shook it off and rolled into Chana, hoping to unbalance her again, but Chana deftly hopped over her and settled into a fighting stance along one side of the mat.

Sigrid pushed herself upright and mirrored the pose. A stitch in her side pulled her up short, right where Chana had smacked her, and the first prickle of fear tightened her spine.

Damn it. She didn't need this now, not when she was beginning to wear Chana down.

Chana took two running steps and leapt into the air, her baston raised high. Her face was set in a rigid mask, fierce and determined, and Sigrid's heart pattered into double time. She scrambled back as she raised her baston. Chana's came down hard, slapping rattan against rattan, and Sigrid's baston twisted down, slipping out of her grip. She fumbled it as Chana immediately reversed her swing and stabbed at Sigrid's side, exactly where she'd hit before, and Sigrid slapped the baston away with her free hand, nearly losing her hold on her own baston in the process.

A sharp inhale caught her attention. Not Will. He had too much discipline to show emotion during such a crucial fight.

The inhale came again, and horror swept through her. Her breath, *hers*, ragged and harsh in her throat, like the irregular gallop of her heart in her chest.

She was going to lose.

Chana pressed on, her baston swinging in alternating sweeps with her free hand. Thrust, slap, sweep, lunge, forcing Sigrid around the mat, and Sigrid's parries grew ever more panicked.

He would be lost to her forever.

Her heel hit the edge of the mat, and she teetered there, reeling away from Chana's rapid fire blows, deflecting them as best she could, and still they came, relentlessly.

Will gone, nevermore hers through the long, lonely centuries ahead.

Chana double tapped the baston against Sigrid's shoulder, numbing it, then backstabbed the grip end into Sigrid's chest.

"Point, Chana," the judge called, and Sigrid froze.

Out of the corner of her eye, she caught sight of Will standing steadfast, his feet spread wide against the gym's painted floor, his arms crossed over his chest, his leaf green eyes shuttered. No emotion stained his expression, nor taughtened his muscles, but it was there. She could almost taste it, a smooth sweetness under the acrid fear coating her mouth.

Her heart squeezed tight in her chest, flipped over, and in that moment, something she had felt only rarely trickled into her, and she found her balance, found her strength in the purpose he'd given her, in the love he shared.

In the love she'd found with this man, this beautiful, gentle man who'd tamed her even as she'd sought to tame him.

Her focus homed in on Chana, razor sharp, and she lunged forward, shoving Chana away. Chana stumbled backward along the mat, and Sigrid pressed her advantage, following with a flurry of quick, light strikes. Shoulder, wrist, hip, arm. Chana scrambled to defend herself, easily evading the blows even as she regained her balance, but Sigrid would not be put off this time. She had something to gain, something to win for, a drive she'd never before had in all her long life, a motivation beyond the ingrained, instinctive will to survive.

She calculated each blow, placing them squarely where they would do the most accumulated harm, and struck when Chana's defenses left her vulnerable, a clear double tap to Chana's sternum.

"Points, Sigrid," the judge said. "Challenge met."

Sigrid backed away immediately, her shoulders heaving under every breath. She met Chana's gaze evenly and bowed. "Well met, kaetyrm."

Chana's expression flashed through a series of subtle shifts, then a small smile tugged at her mouth. She cupped her hands into a fist over the baston and bowed. "Well met, Sigrid Deathknell. I wish you well."

"And you, Chana."

They turned in near unison and bowed to the judge, who returned their salutation, then strong hands turned Sigrid gently around, and there he was, the man whose daring had captured her heart.

"Hey," he said, his voice gruff. "You ok?"

"I'm fine, Will. I—" She swallowed down the words crowding her throat and arched an imperious eyebrow. "This is not how a Son greets the woman who's won him in combat."

His lips quirked into a half smile. "Screw that, honey."

He yanked her against his chest and wrapped his arms

around her, and his mouth came down on hers, hard and demanding, claiming her there in front of his family and hers. The baston slid out of her hand and she curled her fingers into his waist, holding him, giving everything in her heart as whispers rose around them and Will's arms tightened on her and someone nearby coughed politely.

He eased away, breaking the kiss, and touched his forehead to hers. "We'll talk about how not traditional we're going to be later, ok?"

She nodded, unable to contain a happy grin. "We'll talk, yes."

A soft hand touched Sigrid's shoulder, almost lost among the throbbing bruises. Sigrid forced her gaze away from Will, and found his youngest sister standing beside them, her expression drawn into a troubled frown.

"Mom," Casey whispered, then Wilhelmina marched up to them, her husband in tow, and by the fury tautening the other Daughter's posture, Sigrid needed only one guess as to exactly what was on Wilhelmina's mind.

Eighteen

Will took his time turning around to greet his mother, and kept one hand firmly on Sigrid's arm. The way he figured it, she was his now, won fair and square, and screw anybody who got between them. If his mom wanted to join that group, so be it.

When he finally turned around, Wilhelmina's icy fury betrayed itself in the hot glare of her gaze. He sighed and flicked a glance at his dad. "There's a room set up for challenge mediation."

Troy nodded and opened his mouth to speak.

Wilhelmina shook her head, interrupting him. "There's nothing to mediate here."

"Willie," Troy said, a warning note in his voice.

Will clenched his teeth together. "We're making a scene, not to mention that there are more challenges coming up, including one between the director and Lukas Alexiou."

Wilhelmina's jaws snapped shut. "Very well."

Will threaded his fingers through Sigrid's and silently lead the small group away, weaving around the teenagers readying to clean the mat for the next match. The murmurs of the people crowding the bleachers faded into a dull roar by the time they reached the room near the men's locker room, normally reserved for visiting coaches. The outer door snicked shut, silencing the crowd, highlighting the squeak of their shoes against the waxed floor.

Will opened the mediation room's door and held it as Casey, Sigrid, and his parents filed inside, then closed it and leaned back against it, his arms crossed over his chest.

Wilhelmina took three steps into the room and whirled on him, seemingly unmindful of the tight fit of their group among a row of lockers to one side, a desk against one wall, and two chairs in front of it.

"This is unacceptable," she said. "I'm asking for a rematch."

Will shrugged one shoulder. "You can try."

Sigrid cut a silencing glance at him. "On what grounds?"

"The unsuitability of the match." Wilhelmina tossed her head back, sending her dark blonde curls flying around her shoulders. "The inability of the winner to meet my terms."

Will dropped his hands to his sides. "What terms?"

His mother's mouth tightened. "She knows."

"I agreed to meet your conditions prior to the challenge," Sigrid said evenly. A thin thread of fatigue underscored the words. "What more do you want?"

"All of it." The words were nearly spat out. "Everything you have, and full physical Retribution when you discard him."

Fury whipped through Will. He shoved himself away from the door and in two strides stood toe to toe with his mother. "Fuck that, Mom. I'd rather walk out right now than submit her to Retribution."

Wilhelmina smiled coldly. "Then walk out."

Sigrid's already pale skin leeched of color. "Will."

He shook his head. "If that's what she wants, that's what she'll get. C'mon."

He held his hand out to Sigrid. Her eyes widened, so blue, they nearly glowed. "You don't know what you're doing, Will."

"Oh, I'm well aware."

He left his hand hanging in the air between them, his gaze glued to his mother's, and waited. Wilhelmina thrust her chin out, her shoulders stiff and ungiving as Casey clasped her hands together at her waist and bit her lip, worrying it between white teeth.

Troy placed a gentle hand on his wife's shoulder, then glanced at Will. "Do what you have to, son."

"I am, Dad." Will wiggled his fingers at Sigrid and deliberately softened his voice. "Come on, honey. Let me take you home and tend to those bruises."

Sigrid hesitated, her mouth a thin line in her face, and for a moment Will's heart flipped over in his chest and unease tightened his skin. Would she really turn him down after winning the challenge with Chana? Would she really forsake him now, when he'd thrown his mother's ridiculous demands in her face?

Finally, Sigrid placed her hand in his, and relief whooshed out of him in a silent sigh.

"I'll have my lawyer contact Anya early next week to draw up the contract," she said.

Wilhelmina's mouth trembled once, then firmed, and her expression blanked. "Don't bother. I have no son to negotiate for."

Casey sucked in a breath, and Troy said, "Willie, don't," but his mother shook his hand off and turned her back on Will.

Something inside him died in that moment, hope that she'd finally see him as the man he was, and had been for well over a decade, or maybe the last yearning a son had to earn his mother's respect.

Whatever brand of hurt it was, he tucked it away. There'd be plenty of time later to examine it in full. He pulled Sigrid into the curve of his body, shielding her from his mother's hatred the only way he could. "Casey, you know what to do at The Omega. Dad."

Troy shook his head as he stepped forward and clapped a hand to Will's shoulder, and the embrace said everything neither man could say, sharing a love so deep, words could never fully express it.

It'll be ok.

Will wasn't so sure. He nodded once, then opened the door and lead Sigrid away from the family he'd once thought so strong, only death could tear it apart.

REBECCA STOOD on the mat facing her opponent, the leader of the Shadow Enemy, if only in name. A judge stood to her left, and hadn't that been a hard task, finding someone among the People who would fairly judge a challenge involving young Lukas? Who among them did not hate the Shadow for the brutal slaughter of centuries past, for the deaths gouged out of the People's number? Family, friends, loved ones, all sacrificed in a feud stretching back millennia.

She'd found neutrality in an unlikely source suggested by Hawthorne: The Councilmember's house-bound niece, a former Councilmember, and a member of the subversive Eternal Order, Isolde Zellinger.

Never would Rebecca have trusted such a Daughter to judicially mediate a dispute between younglings over a beloved toy, let alone a challenge of such import the outcome could reverberate through both the People and the Shadow for generations to come. Yet here they were, facing that exact situation.

Isolde stepped forward, a hanbō in each hand, and began the proceedings. Rebecca forced her attention there, on the ceremonial rigmarole so necessary for the maintenance of tradition. She ached for it to be over and done with, so she could return to her husband's side and the comfort of his love.

When had she become so tired of it all, of her duty to the People, of the traditions handed down from time immemorial, of the fight she herself often spearheaded?

The Shadow approaches and the Blade must yield

She staunched the shudder automatically rising within her, but only just. The Woman spoke true, of that Rebecca had no doubt, but today was not the day for the Blade's demise. Lukas would never dare go beyond the bounds of the challenge and kill her, not when his very life would be forsaken at the hands of the People assembled as witnesses.

Not when his beloved nephew's life was at risk.

And Lukas was weakened today by his recent ordeal at the hands of his brother and uncle. He lacked the strength to win the challenge, let alone to kill a Daughter of Rebecca's skill.

No, today was not the day the Woman had foreseen. That time rested in the future, beyond the here and now that must first be dealt with.

Lukas restated the challenge he'd issued to her only days past, Isolde laid out the standard terms of contact and handed them the hanbōs, and Rebecca dutifully tested the one given her. She fought today not for herself, but on behalf of the People, something she would do well to remember.

Rebecca finished testing the hanbō and nodded at Isolde, then waited politely until Lukas did the same.

"Begin," Isolde said, and her voice held the regal ring of authority it always had, free of the imprisonment she'd faced over the past few months.

Lukas nodded at Rebecca, a respectful salute. He rotated his wrist, swinging the hanbō in a small circle, and stepped cautiously to his left, his gaze fixed on Rebecca.

Slow and easy then. She mirrored his steps, carefully tracking his movements around the mat. Whatever his strategy, it was obscured by the hard set of his blue eyes in a face so cold, it could've been chiseled from ice. It wasn't determination she saw there so much as grit, and that worried her a bit. Determination was fueled by needs of the moment, but grit was in it for the long haul. Grit created future goals and stuck by them long enough to see them accomplished.

What was Lukas hoping to gain here? What was his long-term goal?

Nala.

The answer hit her even as he swung out and swiped the end of the hanbō through the air a mere half inch in front of her stomach. She swiped the testing blow away, unrattled by the almost leisurely swish as it passed by.

Was he toying with her?

She lunged into a thrust aimed for the soft part of his torso, just below where the two sides of his ribcage met. He stepped back on one foot, dodging the blow, and pushed the tip of her hanbō aside with his free hand, then swiveled around and swung the hanbō in a backhanded arc toward her exposed ribs.

Not toying, then.

She spun away from the blow, out of reach, and settled into a ready stance. This time, he mirrored her, even going so far as to switch the hanbō to his opposite hand, so that they were, in a way, exact mirror images. Light and dark, good and evil, or perhaps both were subjective. Perhaps he thought himself the good here, the light, despite his role as the lead of an organization that had, for millennia, tried to eradicate her kin one brutal murder at a time.

Around the mat they went, slowly revolving around each other as the crowd's quiet murmurs stilled and silence fell around them. A testing blow here, a feint there, but it was gentle, like the first snowfall in early winter, when the ground was still warm from the summer's sun.

This could last all night.

Rebecca parried a thrust, twisting her hanbō around Lukas's in an attempt to disarm him. He easily countered and danced back, hanbō in hand, and she blew out a breath. It was time for this to end, time for young Lukas to receive his comeuppance.

She was going to let him stay.

The thought echoed in the back of her mind as she attacked, vicious now in a sharp contrast to the almost leisurely blows they'd been trading. It was time to end the challenge, but whether he won or not, he was too valuable to let go. He'd been right the day he'd issued the challenge. The People needed him as a go between with the Oracle. He knew her too well, knew too much about her, to risk having him wander about on his own, unprotected, following his own agenda.

He'd earned Rebecca's respect here in a way she'd never expected.

But she must best him today, for the sake of every Daughter and Son who had fallen at the hands of him and his forbears. Justice must be met.

Still, she tempered her blows, refusing to strike hardest where he was most vulnerable. Humiliation wasn't the aim here, merely defeat, and that could be accomplished with honor, as she had always fought. As she'd taught her own daughters and granddaughters, and the many, many others she'd counseled or taught or lead over the long, long centuries of her life.

It was time to end this.

And so, she did.

Three minutes after her real attack began, after a dizzying array of strikes Lukas had barely been able to counter, if at all, and two points earned for her part, Rebecca caught him in a rare defenseless moment, when his body was turned slightly away from countering a thrust, and swiped the hanbō against the back of his legs. His feet flew out from under him and he landed flat on his back.

Quickly, she tapped his chest lightly with the end of her hanbō, then stepped back. "Do you yield, Shadow?"

He rolled over on his side and onto his knees, and to his credit, not a single groan issued from his throat. He placed the hanbō across his thighs and looked up at her, pride shining from his eyes in place of the defeat she'd expected to see.

A burst of whispers in the bleachers interrupted his answer. Rebecca glanced around and located the disturbance. The Oracle, followed by four Handmaidens, was stepping calmly down from the seat she'd assumed at the beginning of the first match earlier in the evening.

Lukas sighed, and when Rebecca looked back at him, his

head hung low and his shoulders were slumped. He rubbed a hand over his sweat soaked hair, ruffling it into dark spikes, then looked up at her, and his expression was no longer that of a proud warrior, but one of a man facing certain hardship.

He opened his mouth, pressed his lips together into a thin line, then said, "Take care of Stephen."

She arched a single eyebrow. "I thought that's what we were settling here."

Lukas shook his head. "Take care of him if Nala kills me."

"What?"

"She's done it before, so many times." He laughed, low and bitter, and closed his eyes tight. "Probably will again."

The Oracle stepped onto the mat, startling Rebecca out of her confusion over his answer, and walked straight to Lukas. The Oracle said something in her guttural, oddly familiar language. Lukas responded with a single word, then she slapped him hard and spoke again, her voice so dispassionate, chills ran down Rebecca's spine.

She tightened her grip on the hanbō, ready to step in. Domestic violence was unacceptable, whatever form it took. She would not allow anyone to abuse an individual under her care regardless of the sins he'd committed. Battle was one thing, attacking a defeated man something else entirely.

Lukas held a hand up, though whether he meant it as a plea to the Oracle or to Rebecca, she couldn't say. He spoke in a low voice in the Oracle's language. Nala shook her head once, then he glanced up at her and Rebecca nearly gasped. His cheeks were red and the muscles of his neck and arms were pronounced, as if he were holding himself in check.

"Tell them who you are," he gritted out, and when the Oracle shook her head again, he screamed, "Tell them!"

The Oracle stood there for a moment gazing down at him, then at long last, she spoke in the same, indecipherable language she'd been using.

Lukas laughed wearily and hung his head, his rage abruptly

gone. "In English, Nala. *English.*"

The Oracle tilted her head up, chin high, and said, "I am Abragni, the Light of the People and the youngest of the Seven."

The hanbō slid from Rebecca's grasp and thudded onto the mat, and she sank down behind it, her legs suddenly too weak to hold her weight. "Abragni?" she whispered, and the name was echoed around the gymnasium, over and over again until it built into a roar that was a single name, obliterating the sounds of the attendees rising from where they sat and filing down onto the floor. Soon, a circle of people spread out around Abragni, kneeling down as close to her as they could.

A Sister, alive. After all this time.

The Oracle slid her fingers into Lukas's hair, stroking gently. She glanced around at Rebecca, her expression like stone. "He will stay."

Rebecca bowed, touching her forehead to the cool mat on which she knelt. Yes, Lukas would stay, and not just for his own sake or that of the boy bound to his care. How could she possibly turn away the mate of her own progenitor, the last surviving member of the Seven Sisters and a founder of the People?

The Light.

Rebecca eased upright as the Prophecy floated through her mind. All along, they'd had its key hidden here within the refuge she'd helped create, and now, the pieces were falling into place one by one.

It was a good time to be alive, she thought, and stood, as the leader she was, to officially welcome this oldest member of the People back into their fold.

Nineteen

After the last match, Sigrid allowed Will to lead her out of the gym and home. They'd caught the tail end of the Blade's challenge match with the Shadow. What a revelation that had been. Will had stood stock still beside her at the opening of the locker room as people flowed past them onto the floor where Abragni stood, her hand on Alexiou's dark head.

A Sister, alive. How could that possibly be?

Sigrid shoved aside the impossibility of a human body surviving for nearly ten millennia. The curse trumped basic biology. Hadn't she learned that first hand, as her own life extended into century after long century?

At home in her bedroom, Will gently tugged off her clothes and his, then urged her into a hot shower and washed her, his hands tender on her bruised skin.

"The fight was rough on you," he murmured.

She rotated a sore shoulder, shrugging his words off. "No more than usual."

He slid a soap-lathered washcloth under her breasts, across her stomach, and in spite of the stiffness in her body, in spite of the cuts and bruises and the awful aftermath of the challenge, heat flared to life within her.

She turned abruptly, crossed her forearms against the shower's wall, and rested her forehead on them. Her heart ached for Will, for the loss she'd known he would suffer. How could a mother forsake her own son? And over a woman, no less. It was unthinkable, and there was nothing Sigrid could do about it.

And so, her heart filled with sorrow and teetered on the edge of breaking, something it had never done.

Will scrubbed her back, rinsed her off. Tugged the showerhead out of its holder and washed her hair, then washed himself quickly, while she leaned against the wall, sorting through her own emotions.

"Come here," he said, so low she almost missed it, then she was in his arms under the hot spray, nestled against his bare chest, hiding the tears she'd never shed over a man in the hollow of his throat.

How could she ever face him, now that she'd caused such a huge rift between him and his family?

His hand cupped the back of her head and he pressed a kiss to her forehead. "Shh. It'll be ok. You'll see."

"How?"

The word slipped out, muffled against his skin. His arms tightened around her, solid, strong. "You'll see," he repeated, and ushered her out of the shower into a soft, fluffy towel.

She watched him while he cared for her, drying her off, tending bruises and cuts, sliding a loose t-shirt over her head. He towel-dried her hair, twisted it into a loose braid. His spring green eyes remained hidden behind a tightly fixed expression.

"You're staring," he said, breaking the silence that had fallen between them.

"Mmm." She reached out to him and caught his hand, and kissed his palm. "You're quiet."

"Not a lot to say."

"Do you want to talk about it?"

"What's to talk about?" He opened the bathroom door and strode out, and was back in a moment wearing a clean pair of underwear. "Bedtime."

A laugh huffed out of her on a soft breath of air. "I'm not a child."

"You've had a rough night." He took her hands in his and helped her stand, pulling her against his chest. "Maybe I need to hold you."

She sighed against his chest and relaxed into him. "That sounds lovely."

"I've wanted to, for so long. Wanted to hold you, love you, fuck you."

He laughed, but there was a bitter undertone to it, an emotion Sigrid couldn't quite put her finger on. She eased back and glanced up at him, studying him beneath the fringe of her eyelashes. "Talk to me, Will."

"And say what? That I'm sorry my mom couldn't accept the woman I lo—?" He bit the word off, then heaved a sigh so heavy, Sigrid's heart broke all over again. "In bed with you now, my beautiful warrior."

"If you insist," she said, aiming for a lighter tone, and missed it by a mile.

He loved her.

She shook her head as she climbed dutifully into bed and settled against her pillow. No, she'd misheard surely. Will wouldn't hold something like that back, would he? Not now, when he needed her support the most.

Yet he cut off the light and climbed into bed without another word, and settled down beside her so far away, only his hand touched her where he draped it over her hip.

"Will," she said softly into the darkness stretching between them. "Come to me."

He shifted on the bed, and his knee grazed her thighs. "You need rest."

No, she needed *him*. The thought struck her hard, slicing right through the sorrow, carrying a hope she'd tried to deny for so long.

Will could break her curse, but in the doing, he would lose his family.

She lay there for a long while, torn between hope and sorrow and a rising tide of emotion she scarcely recognized. In her torment, she shifted on the bed and curled into him, needing him now as she'd never needed another man. "Make love to me, Will."

"Sigrid," he said, his voice strained. "You were barely able to walk out of the gym under your own steam."

True enough. The bout had taken a lot out of her, physically and emotionally, but the stiffness was fading already, replaced by a growing urgency to bind him to her while she could, to have this moment with him before he came to his senses and realized what he was giving up to be with her.

She slid her fingertips down his chest, reveled in the sharp breath he hissed in, and delved under the waistband of his underwear. He was warm there, rigid under her touch, and so very, very tempting.

"Sigrid, come on."

She tightened her hand around his erection and stroked downward, once. "Please, Will. I need you."

"Fuck," he said, but there was no rancor in his voice. He wiggled out of his underwear and tossed them aside. His mouth found hers in the dark shadows sliding across her bedroom, and that emotion surged upward again, breaking through every barrier she'd erected against him and the world waiting so eagerly to destroy her and every Daughter like her.

She gave in to him, kissing him back with a thirst she hadn't felt in so long, she'd nearly forgotten it, and in that moment, the name of that emotion came to her, like a bolt of lightning in the midst of a storm.

Love.

She nearly laughed then, nearly shouted it out for him to hear. She loved him, deeply, truly, so much it hurt to think it, knowing her love would tear him in two. His sacrifice was larger than her own, and yet how could she give him up, when he was the key to her happiness, to her heart?

Will rolled over onto his back, taking her with him, and she slid over him, silently sharing her love in the only way she could, with her touch and her kiss and her acceptance of him in every corner of her soul.

THE NEXT DAY, Will got up early and tended to Sigrid's scrapes, the ones that hadn't healed in spite of her immortal juju, then made her breakfast and tried to avoid talking about the elephant in the room, his An-cursed mother.

As soon as he'd settled Sigrid on the couch with a mug of hot chocolate and a good book, he slipped away and drove the short distance to his grandmother's house.

He gritted his teeth and tightened his grip on the truck's steering wheel. Damn his pride. No way was he standing for his mother's poor treatment of Sigrid, or of him. A Son had rights among the People. Sure, he could stand aside and let his mother ostracize him and Sigrid both, but damn it, he loved the ornery cuss too much not to mend the rift if he could.

He loved his family, so he had to try.

Anya met him at her front door dressed in her usual weekend attire, also her usual weekday attire, a peasant blouse over faded jeans. As soon as she saw him, she sighed and stepped back, then closed the door behind him against the cold. "I've already heard."

He shrugged out of his jacket and hung it on the peg fastened to the wall behind the door. "Good. That'll save a lot of time."

"She's hellbent on disinheriting you. Sent me an email last night letting me know I needed to come up with a fitting Retribution for abandoning a Son."

A sharp pang stabbed Will's heart, taking his breath. Already? Did he mean so little to his mother then?

Anya's expression softened and she patted his arm. "There now, child. It's not as bad as all that. You know your mother. Piss and vinegar when she's hurt, and she's hurting now, that's all. She'll come around."

Will frowned. "You weren't there, Amma. She turned her back on me."

"Well, it's not the first time. Headstrong girl turned her back on me, too, once." Anya slid her arm through Will's and tugged. "Come. I've a fire going in the library. We can sit in front of it and chat like we used to when you were a tiny tot playing with your wooden cars at my feet."

A memory flashed through his mind, of a roaring fire and roasting marshmallows, of Anya's silver braids swinging as she smiled down at his younger self, her cornflower blue eyes twinkling. Some of his hurt eased and he managed a laugh. "I'm a little old for toys."

"Not too old for a chat, though."

"Never that," he murmured, and walked with her through the house he'd always loved into her kitchen, where she pulled out milk and cocoa and set to making hot chocolate.

Will leaned a hip against the counter beside her, watching her bustle here and there as the milk heated and she readied two enormous mugs. "Planning for a long chat?"

"Of course. We haven't had one in a long while."

He shifted against the counter, crossed his arms over his chest. "Do you think it's going to take that long to come up with a way to stop Mom from going nuts?"

"Oh, that happened a long time ago," Anya said, smiling.

"I'm not asking you to do all the work. Just...help me." He shrugged, suddenly uncomfortable there in the heart of her home. "Maybe act as a mediator so we can sort this out. I don't want to lose my family."

"But you will," she said, her blue eyes sharp, "if Willie forces your hand."

Will pressed his lips together into a tight line. His grandmother knew her family too well. "I have a right to live my life the way I see fit."

"Only if it accords with your mother's wishes." The words were gentle, as pointed as they were. "It's the woman, I think. If you had fallen in love with someone else—"

He shook his head, impatient. "I knew as soon as I saw Sigrid that she was the one for me."

"Your grandfather was the same way. Always so certain. He swept me off my feet with his bright charm and brighter eyes. Just like yours. Oh, not the color, no, but the shape. The laughter and love and determination." She clucked her tongue and turned to the milk simmering on the stove. "Broke my curse before I knew it, and now look where I'm at."

"Happy," Will said, and she grinned up at him, her expression mischievous.

"Only when it suits me." Her grin faded into a sigh and she snapped the stove's eye off. "I'll act as your mediator, Will, but I won't interfere. I can't change Willie's mind, now that it's set."

And well he knew it, but still. He had to try. "Thanks, Amma. You're the best."

She harrumphed and arched her eyebrows high. "Don't I know it. Now, get down those cookies from the top shelf and we'll have ourselves a treat."

Obediently, he snagged the cookies she kept hidden on a shelf so high, she needed a ladder to fetch them. A deterrent, she said, to keep her from overindulging.

"Good matches last night," she said, and Will sighed, relieved over her easy acceptance. The battle lay ahead of him, but here was an ally, one he'd sorely need when he faced off with his mother and tried to force her to see reason.

Twenty

Early Monday morning, Sigrid woke with Will wrapped around her. She lay there for a moment, still half asleep, reveling in the warmth of his body against hers.

Today they confronted his mother.

She burrowed her head into the pillow and shoved the worry aside. There was plenty of time for that later, just not now in the remnants of a weekend spent with the man she loved.

Will sighed into her hair and his hips shifted against hers. He grunted and buried his face in her nape, and the hard length of his arousal pressed against her ass. "Mmm. I love waking up next to you."

A small smile played around the corners of her mouth. "You want sex."

"Damn skippy. C'mere, woman."

But she didn't have to. His hands tugged her panties down and pushed her onto her belly, and he slid into her slick heat, loving her until they both panted their releases out into the bedroom's early morning chill.

Later, after breakfast and a shower, Sigrid chose her clothes carefully, oddly numb around the lump growing in her stomach.

Will slumped on the edge of her bed, buttoning a crisp, white dress shirt over an equally white t-shirt, his expression calm.

She placed a hand over her stomach and closed her eyes. Where was her own calm, so readily at hand through battles and matings and the odd politics inherent to any gathering among the People?

Lost, she feared, under the stress of the past few weeks.

Her fingers clenched into a knot against the raw silk dress she wore, and the lump in her stomach leapt into her throat, lodging there.

What was she going to do, now that she'd discovered her heart?

Warm hands cupped her shoulders and drew her back against Will's solid length. "I love that dress."

She half turned toward him, her head bowed. "Thank you."

"You look stunning in red." His hands slid down her arms and landed on her hips, and he pressed a kiss to the side of her throat. "You look stunning in anything."

She laughed lightly, tried to. It came out wrong, choked and stunted, not the fearless humor of a warrior well honed.

"Hey, now," he said, and his arms wrapped around her, holding her tight, safe. "It's going to be ok. Trust me."

"I do," she murmured.

"Yeah?"

Always, she thought, but the single affirmation stuck in her throat, unable to escape the fear clogging her voice.

"Mom will back down," Will said. "You'll see."

"And if she doesn't?"

His shrug shifted his shirt against her bare arms. "We'll deal with it, one day at a time."

She closed her eyes and relaxed against him. One day at a time. Such simple ease over the nightmare awaiting them.

Not long after, they bundled up and headed toward Anya's house, the site of the mediation Will had negotiated on Sigrid's behalf, without her being aware of his intent. She'd said not a single, chastising word to him when he'd told her on Saturday night, merely placed her hand over his and quietly asked what she could do.

Anything. That was the least of what she'd do for him.

Wilhelmina and Troy were already there when Will parked Sigrid's car along the curb in front of Anya's house. They exited the vehicle in unison, strode up the sidewalk, her gloved hand in his, their breaths frosting in the icy air.

Snow later, a fitting harbinger to the day's duty.

Anya's little mouse of an assistant greeted them at the door and took their outerwear, then led them to Anya's library. Four chairs were arrayed in front of Anya's Mission Style desk, in groupings of two centered at each front corner of the desk.

Wilhelmina stood facing the fire on the opposite side of the room, Troy at her side. He looked up when Will and Sigrid entered. Wilhelmina did not.

The lump that had been gathering inside Sigrid all morning withered into a tight knot in her chest.

Anya stepped out from behind the desk, a warm smile on her face. "Good morning Will, Sigrid."

Will bent and hugged his grandmother. "Hey, Amma. How's the temperature?"

"Frigid," Anya said, her serious tone a sharp contrast to the soft smile she wore. "Tea, coffee?"

Will glanced at Sigrid and brushed a finger over the end of his nose. "None for us, thanks."

Anya arched a single eyebrow at Sigrid, no doubt over the impropriety of Will answering for them both. Such was a Daughter's duty and right, but Sigrid held her tongue, afraid her own voice would choke before it left her throat.

"Well, then." Anya slipped away from Will and rounded her desk. "Shall we begin?"

"There's nothing to say." Wilhelmina's voice cracked through the room, sharp thunder after the boldest strike of lightning. "He made his choice."

"Yet here we are," Anya said evenly.

"Because you threatened to disown me."

Will crossed his arms over his chest and coughed into his fist, hiding a dimpled smile.

Troy murmured something too low for Sigrid to hear. Wilhelmina huffed out a breath and flounced across the room, her heels as sharp against the ancient rugs lining the library's floor as her anger.

Once they were all settled into chairs, Sigrid and Wilhelmina bracketing the men sitting in the inner chairs, Anya relaxed in her chair and eyed them steadily. "My grandson asked me to mediate the dispute between him and my daughter. I have agreed on the condition that I mediate only. Will, you may begin."

Will turned and looked at his mother, his gaze steady against her icy hot glare. "I love Sigrid more than my own life."

Wilhelmina sucked in a breath and paled, her lips a thin, red slash against her ashen skin.

"She accepted me when she didn't have to, fought for me," Will continued. "Won. By law, I'm hers. There is no choice."

Sigrid's hands tightened painfully on the arms of her chair. She opened her mouth, fully intending to dispute his words. Will was free to leave her, free to live his life as he pleased. She couldn't hold him, wouldn't if it meant hurting him.

Anya lifted a single hand, silencing Sigrid's protest before it began, but it was too late. The knot in Sigrid's stomach shoved upward into her throat and burst inside her, filling her head with the oddest pressure. She placed a hand to the buzzing in her ears, scarcely aware of the conversation eddying around her.

"Even if there were a choice, I would stay with her," Will said. "I love her, but I love you, too, Mom."

"If you loved me," Wilhelmina said stiffly, "you would never have defied me in the first place."

"For fuck's sake," Will muttered. "It's not like we can control who we love."

"You could've tried. You could've had some respect, some consideration, for your mother's opinion, if not your own welfare."

A slow fire sparked in Sigrid's chest, burning under the weight of Wilhelmina's words. She inhaled tentatively, seeking to ease it, and just managed to control the cough tickling her throat before it could interrupt the proceedings.

"Willie," Troy said, and Anya shushed him with a gentle reminder of the People's rules. Women talked. Men obeyed. That's the way it had always been, hadn't it? From the first day of the curse until now, when hope had finally come upon them. The curse could be broken, would be if the stars aligned correctly.

"I love her," Will said, his voice as implacably recalcitrant as his mother's. "Why are you punishing me for finding love? Why can't you be happy for me?"

Wilhelmina stood abruptly, her eyes flashing a fire burning as brightly as the one consuming Sigrid. "She'll be the ruination of you. As soon as she's had her fill, she'll discard you, leaving you an empty husk. How long before she uses you up? I'll not have that for my son."

Sigrid shook her head, a mute denial. She should say something, defend herself, and would if only this blasted buzzing would cease. Will would never be discarded. She could never betray him, never lose him. He was her life, her love, discovered after so long on her own. Why had she ever resisted the idea in the first place?

But she had, and now here he was, her destiny. Surely they could all see that.

"I can take care of myself," Will said hotly.

Wilhelmina slashed a hand through the air, hurt fury radiating out of her stiff posture and fixed expression. "Then take care of yourself, and don't come crawling back to me when she's through with you."

Troy stood, his expression tight with anger. "Don't say

something you'll regret, Willie."

"No," Sigrid said, the single word a counterpoint to his. "I love him."

Will jerked around, his eyes wide. "You what?"

Anya threaded her fingers together over her stomach, a satisfied expression on her face. "I think she said that she loves you."

"When?" Will said. "How?"

Wilhelmina stepped toward them, unmindful of Troy moving to block her path. "She's lying. That cold hearted bitch has never loved anything in her life except her own hide."

Sigrid lifted her head through the thick morass clinging to her and met Wilhelmina's gaze with her own. "I love him, but I won't separate him from his family."

"Fuck that," Will spat out.

Sigrid reached a hand toward him as a tear slipped down her face. Wilhelmina was right, in her own narrow-minded way. Outside of her family and a few close friends, Sigrid had never really loved anyone. She'd never loved a man before, never given her heart. How did she know now that what she felt for Will was real, true, as eternally strong as love should be? How could she wrest him from his family, knowing her own love might falter at some point, leaving him in exactly the situation Wilhelmina so feared?

Better for him not to face that. Far better for him that she not be a part of his life.

"I renounce my claim," she whispered through the noise filling her to the brim. "I renounce—"

The noise ceased, leaving a dread silence behind, and in its wake, a great weight pressed down on Sigrid. She gasped under the pressure, struggling to breathe. Will slid out of his chair and knelt beside her, his forehead creased into a frown. "Sig, honey, what's wrong?"

His words were thin, distant. She clutched a hand around his forearm and said, "Love you," then the weight lifted suddenly, carrying her up with it until she could go no higher, and she separated from it and fell down alone, lost in a world without her Will.

WILL SCRAMBLED out of his chair and knelt beside Sigrid, ignoring his mother's squawking, his father's attempts to calm her, and his grandmother's satisfied smirk. That last especially. The old biddy had played them all, though to what end he had no clue.

He shoved the thought aside and gently patted Sigrid's cheek. She'd been acting strange all morning, since the end of the exhibition, truth be told, but today more so. And now she slumped in her chair, her hands like ice and her pulse rapid under his fingertips.

Damn it, what was wrong? Daughters didn't get sick. Their immortality protected them from almost everything. Her body had nearly healed after the fight, so what could it be? There was nothing else to explain this sudden collapse.

"Leave her be, dear." Anya knelt beside him and gently pried his fingers away from Sigrid's wrist. "She'll come around in a minute. They always do."

"Come around?" he asked.

Behind him, something thumped heavily into one of the chairs. "I don't believe it," Wilhelmina whispered. "She was telling the truth."

Will clenched his teeth together. "Would somebody please clue me in?"

"She submitted." Anya threaded her arm through Will's and leaned her head against his shoulder. "Her curse is no more, thanks to you."

Will sat back on his heels and stared at Sigrid, at a loss. She loved him, so much she'd somehow submitted to him and broken her curse?

She loved *him*?

"Holy shit," he finally managed, and his grandmother laughed and said, "Yes, that about sums it up."

He shook his head, disentangled himself from his grandmother, and, still ignoring his mother, now deep in a muttered conversation with his father, Will picked Sigrid up, cradling her against his chest, and carried her upstairs to the bedroom he'd used as a child. The room was exactly as he remembered it. Twin beds stood on either side of the room's only window, overlooking the back yard. Matching cedar lined trunks hulked at their feet. Blue and red plaid bedspreads covered the mattresses, an exact match for the curtains tied away from the light spilling into the room through the solitary window.

Will stepped inside the room, skirting a rocking chair and the lone chest of drawers, and placed Sigrid gently on top of one bed. He dug a crocheted afghan out of one of the trunks and draped it over her, then shut the door and pulled the rocking chair up to the side of her bed.

And waited.

Anya's assistant came by offering him a drink. Will waved her away and thought seriously about locking the door, and regretted not doing so when his mother slipped into the room half an hour later and perched on the edge of the other bed.

Will kept right on doing what he was doing, watching Sigrid while rubbing slow circles over her stockinged ankle under the afghan.

Wilhelmina cupped her hands together on her lap, her posture rigid. "How is she?"

"The same," Will said.

"She'll wake in a while."

Will grunted.

Wilhelmina pressed her lips together, shook her head once. After a while, she said, "I'm sorry."

Will glanced at her, sharply. "Why?"

She shrugged, lifted her hands in a helpless gesture, let them fall onto her thighs. "I was wrong about her."

"Yeah, well." Will bit his tongue, staunching the bitter flow of words crowding into his mouth. "You could've believed in me."

"I do, Will."

"Really." The word fell flatly between them, and Wilhelmina flinched. Will soldiered on, determined to get out what he should've said years ago. "I'm a grown man, have been for a long time. You made sure of that, you and Dad."

She turned her face away from him, toward the sunlight softening under the clouds darkening the sky. "It's our way."

"Yeah, that's my point. It's the People's way to breed strong Sons, but you, you left me here to run The Omega and raise Casey, and I did. I did everything you asked. I did it without complaining, without once mentioning that maybe I had something different in mind for my life."

"Will," she said softly, and he rushed on, afraid if he stopped, he'd never speak again.

"I did that because you asked it of me. I did it because I loved you so much, I would've done anything for you. Anything, Mom. And in return, when I finally found somebody I loved as much as I loved you, you tried to come between us. Threatened to disown me. Turned your back on me." He fixed his gaze on the even rise and fall of Sigrid's chest, and swallowed down the bitterness coating his throat. "You were the one who abandoned me."

"Will." The word trembled and broke. Wilhelmina touched her fingers to her mouth and two tears streaked down her cheeks. "I'm sorry, baby, so sorry. I didn't realize you felt that way, that you wanted something different. Why didn't you say anything?"

He shrugged, uncomfortable now that the words were out. He could've been kinder, maybe should've been, but how? How could he have cushioned his mother from the truth, when it was so hard and harsh inside him?

Wilhelmina slid off the bed and knelt beside the one Sigrid lay on. She rested a hand over his, on top of the afghan, stilling his movement. "I always thought we could tell each other anything. When did we stop doing that?"

"I don't know."

He shook his head, trying to pinpoint the moment they'd stopped talking. Had it been when he'd taken over The Omega at sixteen, or later, when his parents had embarked on their world tour, leaving him and Casey here to depend on each other?

What did it matter now? The past was gone, over and done. There was nothing he could do about it now.

He sighed and dropped his hand, and looked straight at his mother for the first time in a long while. Fine lines were etched around her eyes, laugh lines, he hoped, and a few strands of silver shot through her hair. She was no longer a proud immortal Daughter of the line of Abragni, but a mortal wife and mother, *his* mother.

And he loved her.

He stood and leaned across Sigrid, and pressed a kiss to his mother's forehead. "We'll work on that."

Her fingers tightened on his hand and she laughed, low and soft. "Yes, we will. I'll leave you to your duties now. We'll have a feast tonight, to celebrate. A Daughter has found her heart, and my son has found his."

And those were always cause for rejoicing.

Will sat back down and watched his mother leave the room. As soon as the door shut behind her, he resumed his watch over the woman who had stolen his heart and claimed him as no other could.

SIGRID SLOWLY ROSE through the thick fog clogging her head and woke to a brightly lit, unfamiliar room. Will was sitting beside her, his forearms propped on his thighs, staring at her with the same inscrutable look he'd worn since the end of the challenge.

His eyes met hers, and he slowly leaned back, trailing his palms over his thighs. "You ok?"

She mentally probed the corners of her mind, then ran through a subtle check of her body. "I'm fine. What happened?"

"You passed out." One corner of his mouth quirked into a smile. "Amma said you submitted your will to me."

The statement rose on a question, as if he weren't quite sure his grandmother had the right of it. Sigrid sat up slowly, careful of the muzziness filling her head. Had Will somehow broken her curse, by dint of her submission? But when had that—?

She bit the thought off. When she'd decided to exchange her own happiness for his, of course. What else could explain her fainting when she was largely healed and otherwise hale and whole?

Will touched her knee, let his hand fall away. "You scared me."

"Oh, Will. No. I'm fine." She sighed and slipped off the bed into his lap, and curled up there like a kitten at naptime. "We're fine. Aren't we?"

His arms came around her and he tucked her head under his chin. "Yeah. Mom quit bitching when you passed out."

"Every cloud has a silver lining," Sigrid murmured.

He huffed out a short laugh. "If you say so."

"What happened? My memory is a little fuzzy."

"The usual. Blustering and fussing, a lot of accusations. Then you scared the ever loving hell out of me." He pressed a lingering kiss to her forehead. "Don't ever do that to me again."

"I think that's a one time thing."

"For any reason," he amended firmly. "I carried you up here. Mom followed a little later, probably after Dad calmed her down and the shock of seeing a Daughter as strong as you faint had passed. We hashed it out. She's backing down."

The finality of his words worried her. There was more there, she was sure, but wheedling it out of him could wait for another day, when things were running a little more smoothly.

And they would run smoothly. Of that she was certain. Now if she could only get him to tell her he loved her, here in this quiet room with no one watching.

Trust was a two way street, one it was past time they trod together.

She closed her eyes, gathered her courage, and finally said, "I love you, Will."

His arms tightened around her and his breath whooshed out, warming her skin. "Yeah, I figured."

She waited for him to continue, for him to reciprocate, for something. After a long moment, he laughed softly, lifted her chin, and kissed her, slowly, tenderly. Her hands curled into his shirt and held him close as her heart tripped into a jog and she silently begged him to say it, to just tell her how he felt.

At last, he drew back and met her gaze evenly. "I love you, Sigrid, maybe since the first time I saw you, maybe since that day you and Moira got into an argument for the hundredth time and I lost my temper."

"And you kissed me. I remember."

"It's a helluva cute meet."

Giddiness rose in her and laughter followed, spilling out of her in a mad rush to share this rare jubilation with the world. Will loved her, and she loved him. Wasn't that something?

He jiggled her in his arms, a grin slowly growing on his face. "This isn't a laughing matter, woman."

"Oh, Will. If you only knew." Her laughter petered out and she cupped his hand against her cheek. "Where do we go from here?"

"Well, now that you've despoiled me—"

She choked on another laugh and her eyes widened. "Will!"

"I figure the least you can do is make an honest man of me." He leaned down and touched his nose to hers. "What do you say? Do you think we have it in us to master the whole husband and wife gig?"

"I wouldn't have it any other way," she whispered, and

kissed him until he had no doubt whatsoever how much she believed in that very outcome.

Epilogue

The storage room was dark and empty when the Woman with No Face picked the lock and slipped inside. A long table stretched down the middle of the room, supporting five boxes specially made to hold the skeletal remains of a human body.

She shut the door quietly behind herself and flipped on the overhead lights. The work she did tonight required illumination of more than one kind. Light so she could see what she was about, yes, but also a revelation.

The youngest of the Seven, the People's Light, was hidden no more. Slowly, the pieces fell into place one by one, moving the People inexorably toward a time the Woman had witnessed only in visions.

Their future.

She could feel it building within her, suffusing her bones with the same illuminating portent. The stage was set, the players were in place, and she had played her part well. Their time had come, the grand finale the People had anticipated for so long. Now it was left to Abragni to choose a path from among the many spread before her, and the Light would, with the help of the Great Mother, choose the correct way.

Blessed be Ki.

The Woman scrounged through some papers scattered on a table set against the far wall and located a marker. She had so few tasks left, so few visions left to fulfill. This small task, this labeling of the Sisters, she had left as long as she could. She had followed the progress of the women and men working here, encouraging them as she could, but she had foreseen a snag only she could correct: Science would not reveal the identities of the women resting here in these simple boxes. Only the Woman could do so now.

And so she quietly opened each box and discerned which Sister was which, not through any outward marking or sign, but by her inner voice, the Mother Goddess who had guided her for so many millennia. She worked until each box was marked correctly with the name of the Sister it held.

Lilleni. Eleni. Ganenda. Bagda. Marnan.

Five Sisters dead, one revealed, and one still hidden in the shadows.

The Woman closed the boxes and set the pen aside, then stood back and gazed at the boxes as memory pushed through the remnants of visions and war and a life lived too long without the camaraderie of another human being. Yes, it was almost time. Soon, the People would confront their age old enemy and shed the hardships of the past. Soon, she could rest as she had not for so very, very long, rest and perhaps die as she had wished so many times.

That, the Great Lady had never allowed.

The Woman dug a scrap piece of paper out of the untidy pile, sketched her symbol on it, and let it flutter to the floor. Let them know who had solved the mystery here. Let them fear the Woman's coming one last time before the end.

The Woman touched each box in turn, then slipped out of the room, leaving her sisters to the peace they had earned so long ago.

About the Author:
Lucy Varna lives in the Blue Ridge Mountains of northeast Georgia, surrounded by her large, extended family.
Visit her online at:

www.lucyvarna.com
www.daughtersofthepeople.com

The adventure continues...

Redemption
(Daughters of the People, Book 6.5)

Coming soon!

A sneak peek of *Redemption*

Mid-January

India Furia eased the curtain aside a mere fraction and stared out the cabin's window at snow fluttering onto the empty, graveled parking area. Three weeks, she'd been there, trapped in this Ancursed wilderness with no one for company except a herd of deer, the occasional black bear, and, when he could get away, Hiro. Seven weeks since he'd rescued her from the clutches of that goody two shoes Rebecca Upton. Seven weeks since her sister Indigo, beloved above all, had submitted to the Blade's Son and become mortal.

Which of those was more shameful escaped India in that moment. She flicked the curtain into place and paced away from the window's temptation.

Hiro was late.

India stopped in the middle of the living room, her hands opening and closing into hard fists at her side. It's not like she missed him or anything. He'd barely spoken to her since the day she'd woken in Hiro's isolated getaway, handcuffed to his bed like the prisoner Rebecca had tried to make her.

Chained like a common criminal and, worse, confined in one of the cave-like cells hidden away in the deep, dank dark tunneling through the mountain housing the Archives in Tellowee.

India shuddered, shaking off the sheer terror tightening her spine. Never would she be a prisoner, bound by duty or force to the will of another. She'd rather die a hundred deaths.

And had suffered worse escaping just such a fate.

Two seconds later, she was at the window again, peering out into the frigid, late autumn landscape. Snow frosted the grass verging the forest surrounding the mountain cabin. Intrepid cardinals flitted through the pine, flashing hints of color among the grey-green tree trunks. The world outside was silent, serene, and entirely too rural for India's taste.

Blessed Mother, where was he?

Her cellphone buzzed against the rustic coffee table sitting between the couch and the Navajo-patterned blanket thrown over its backrest, and the fire roaring in the woodstove. This phone was the one concession Hiro had made to her many demands for more freedom, the one lifeline she had to the outside world, but only because it led directly to him.

Sneaky bastard had wiretapped the damn thing. No matter who she called or texted, no matter what she did with it, he would know.

And that's what she got for sleeping with a former Delta Forces Operator and current co-owner of a growing personal security business. For all she knew, he had bugs tucked into every nook and cranny of the cabin and was, even now, listening to her pacing back and forth across the oak floors in her socked feet.

The phone buzzed again, yanking her out of her growing irritation. She strode across the room and snatched it up, thumbed into the first text message she'd received, and stopped cold.

Finish it.

Satisfaction flooded into her. She deleted the message, dropped the phone onto the table. The drone of an approaching vehicle fluttered at the edge of her hearing. She crossed to the window and lifted the curtain, spotted Hiro's SUV, and allowed herself a small smile.

Her little interlude with the Blade, and then with her rescuer, hadn't alienated her as she'd feared. The job she'd left unfinished was waiting for her, and she fully intended to see it through, come

Hell or high water, or any force that bitch Rebecca Upton chose to throw at her.

India dropped the curtain and stepped back, affecting an impatient expression for the man who had, for a brief time, been her lover.

Let the games begin.

Coming soon.